Beauty &
the BRUISER

Beauty & the Bruiser

A TYRANTS HOCKEY NOVEL
JOSIE BLAKE

Copyright © 2023 MJB Publications, LLC All rights reserved. This book or any portion thereof may not be reproduced or used in any manner whatsoever without the express written permission of the author except for the use of brief quotations in a book review.

This is a work of fiction. Names, characters, businesses, places, events and incidents are either the product of the author's imagination or used in a fictitious manner. Any resemblance to actual persons, living or dead, or actual events is purely coincidental.

Content edits provided by Jessica Ruddick.

Line editing suggestions provided by Red Adept Editing.

Cover art: Staci Brillhart

ISBN: 978-1-955887-11-3

For all the readers who followed my Chesterboro characters to Philadelphia. Thank you.
Also, this one is for anyone who feels they can't be loved unless they're "perfect." You're just right. Don't ever forget.
And to my three guys, again. Always.

June

"You are aware this is a contract job, correct?" Ms. Raybourne, the communication director of the Philadelphia Tyrants hockey team, looks at me over her reading glasses, a neat gray bun at the base of her neck. "The child's care will end when the hockey season does."

I already answered this question at my first interview. "Absolutely. I hope to get a full-time teaching position next year. The timing works perfectly for me." I offer her a winning smile. "I would just like some flexibility to help my foster mother when she needs me. It should only be during the day—rides to doctors, grocery shopping, things like that."

"You'll have your days to yourself, when the child is in school. She's in the second grade."

"That will be perfect." When Mama Lily had her stroke and fall in the spring, I opted to put off looking for a full-time position. After a few more health setbacks this summer, she's begun to stabilize and make progress, but I want to be available when she needs me.

Ms. Raybourne studies me. Even though my shapewear is cutting off the oxygen to my lungs, I force myself to sit still under her gaze. Tapping her pen on the desk, she glances over my resume again. I don't know what she's looking for. It's only a page long, and she already saw it last week. My college degree and teaching criteria are on top. I graduated from Rutgers University magna cum laude in the spring, so my credentials are nothing to be ashamed of. If she does the math, though, she'll see it took me six years to finish my education. I had to take classes part time and work to pay for it. I got some scholarships, thank goodness. But even with working at the day care part-time, babysitting, and shifts at the diner on weekends, I had to take out loans. Still, not too bad for a foster kid from New Jersey.

She lays the resume on the desk, pushing it away from her. Dread sinks into my gut. Is that the end? I had a feeling this job was too good to be true, but I was still hopeful when I got invited back for a second interview. The pay is extremely generous, more than enough to help me pay off Mama Lily's debts, and it comes with housing. I've been crashing temporarily at friends' houses. I need something more permanent.

As I brace myself for Ms. Raybourne to excuse me, she narrows her eyes. "How do you feel about signing a nondisclosure agreement?"

"I'm sorry?" *Not what I expected.*

She leans back and steeples her fingers. "You're going to live with a professional hockey player. Whatever you see or hear in his home must remain private." Her head tilts. "This includes pictures you take, especially pictures of the child."

I straighten. "I would never share pictures of a child." The suggestion fills me with outrage. Only monsters exploit children. "And my employer's personal life is not my business."

A smile stretches over her lips. "Then you'll sign the NDA? After your attorney looks it over, I mean?"

"Of course," I agree, even though I don't have an attorney or the money to hire one.

"Then you're hired, Miss Harlow." Ms. Raybourne places her palms on the desk, the professional smile still in place.

"I am?"

"As long as Mr. York agrees." Checking her watch, she nods. "He will stop in once practice is over." She raises her eyebrows. "You still want the job, don't you?"

"Well, yes. Absolutely. I wasn't sure..." I don't want to say I didn't think I would get it because that sounds like I shouldn't have it, and I definitely don't want that. Instead, I smile back and offer her my hand. "Yes. I would love the job."

Her grip is firm and not too long, the perfect handshake. Her grin fades, and the seriousness returns to her face. "There's only one more thing, then."

"Yes?"

"I must impress upon you that this is a strictly professional arrangement." She chews on her lower lip. "By that, I mean I need you to conduct yourself professionally and with proper decorum around your employer at all times."

"Proper decorum." *What does that even mean?* "I assure you, Ms. Raybourne, I am the epitome of professionalism. I won't use any inappropriate language, and I'll always dress conservatively around my charge." I pause, searching for other assurances. "Did the headhunter forward my list of references? If you call any of them, they'll testify to my character and decency."

"That's not what I mean, Miss Harlow." She sighs. "Let me be plain. You'll be living with Mr. York, but there shouldn't be any personal relationship between you." When I only blink at her, she elaborates. "Especially not any *physical* relationship."

"Oh," I say, stretching the word out as clarity hits me. My face heats. She can probably make out every freckle I have, and there are a lot of them. "Right. Of course. I get it. Hands off the boss." I grin at her, squaring my shoulders and pretending my skin doesn't match my hair. "I would never."

She leans closer, her tone hushed. "I apologize, but there are a lot of women who would take this role to get closer to someone like Mr. York. Or rather, closer to his seven-figure salary." She shrugs. "It's happened before."

I'm sure it's horror that straightens my spine. I hurry to reassure her and speed along this awkward conversation. "Ms. Raybourne, there's nothing to worry about there. This is a job for me. I love working with kids, and I'm good with them. I started helping with the other foster kids in the homes I've lived in since I went into the system at ten. I've babysat since my early teens, and I've worked in day cares. My degrees are in elementary education and special education. In the future, I'll look for a more permanent position. But this job gives me a chance to do what I love and the flexibility to help my foster mother during a tough time. That's all." I take a breath. "I have no interest in a relationship with Mr. York—no interest in a relationship at all. I certainly have no intention of complicating anything."

That last statement couldn't be truer, and by Ms. Raybourne's genuine smile, she must hear my sincerity. She leans back and taps on the keyboard. "I'll print out the paperwork while we wait for Mr. York to arrive. He said he wanted you to start as soon as possible. Will tomorrow be good for you?"

"Absolutely." I've been staying with my friend Ava for the past week, and her apartment is a closet. She'll be happy to have me out of her hair.

She stands. "Let me just get this stuff off the printer." Sweeping from the room, she leaves the door open.

Alone, I snag my phone from my purse and drop a quick text to Lily. *I got the job!* She responds immediately with a smiley face. I can see Ms. Raybourne through the window next to me, so I pull up my phone's browser and type 'York Philadelphia Tyrants.'

My phone is old and slow, so it takes an embarrassing amount of time for it to load my results.

I know nothing about ice hockey. No one has asked me about my hockey expertise either, so I assume sports knowledge isn't a prerequisite for the job. But since I've never watched a full game, I have no idea who my boss—Mr. York—is. I've heard the stereotypes about hockey players. Hockey's a physical game, and a lot of the players are missing teeth. There's lots of facial hair, too, if I'm not mistaken. I wrinkle my nose.

My search turns up Emmett York. Ms. Raybourne is still at the printer, so I click on the first entry.

I wasn't wrong—there's facial hair. But as I zoom in on the picture, it's not straight mountain man grizzly style but more of a sexy stubble. I find light eyes and a chiseled jaw that even a five o'clock shadow can't hide. Pretty attractive, actually. I click through, and there are action shots of him playing. He's on skates, holding a stick. There's a letter C stitched on his shoulder. Does that mean he's the captain?

"The camera adds ten pounds, they say."

My head twists. Behind me, the tallest man I've ever seen leans against the doorjamb. In a red Tyrants hoodie and black sweats, Emmett York takes up the entire opening. His wet hair falls in his eyes, and there's that stubble on his jaw. The camera wouldn't dare add a thing to this man. If anything, it doesn't do him justice. The picture doesn't hint at the stubborn tilt to his chin or the piercing intensity of his eyes. It definitely doesn't give away how hot he is.

I scurry to my feet as heat blooms on my face. "Um…" I tuck the hand clutching the phone behind my back. "I was just…" Again, words fail. Attempting a bright smile, I square my shoulders and hold out my hand. "Mr. York. Hi. I'm June Harlow."

My hand stays outstretched between us. He grunts, pushing away from the doorjamb, ignoring my gesture. I guess we aren't shaking hands. My hand drops to my side. I start again. "I was just doing some light research."

He stands, legs apart, with his arms crossed. His face is unreadable. "What did you find out?"

"Not much." Reluctantly, I lift my phone and show him the face. "Emmett York. Captain?" My face is still on fire, but I force myself to meet his eyes and lift my eyebrows in question. He nods. "Thought that was what the C meant."

"That's it?" He lifts an eyebrow. "Nothing more interesting?"

"I only had a minute." I click the screen black. "It's just… I don't know anything about hockey or who you are, so I was—"

Ms. Raybourne appears at the door, sifting through a stack of paper. "Here we are. This shouldn't take long… Oh." She stops when she sees Emmett York. "Duke. There you are."

"Yes. Just introducing myself to Ms. Harlow."

"I'm June." I throw in, doing my best to hold my sunniest smile. He gives no noticeable response.

Ms. Raybourne glances between us, obviously sensing the tension, but at a loss to understand what's going on. That makes two of us. Finally, she rallies. "I was about to go through the paperwork with her."

"She agrees to the NDA?" He asks Ms. Raybourne the question, like I'm not in the room.

"I do," I add, because it's rude to talk over people.

He takes the stack of papers from her, still ignoring me. Shuffling through them, he finally nods. "And you realize that this is only for this year?" As I nod, he continues. "And that this is strictly professional. You'll be my daughter's nanny. That's it." He raises his eyebrows at me.

My jaw hurts from clenching. This again? "Yes," I grit out, resisting the urge to roll my eyes.

Ms. Raybourne narrows her eyes. "So... you both agree to the arrangement?" She glares pointedly at Emmett York.

He studies me longer than necessary. Finally, he raps his knuckles on her desk. "She'll do." Turning to the door, he dismisses me. "Email me the paperwork when you're done," he fires over his shoulder as he strides out the door, leaving us both staring at the empty doorway.

"It was nice to meet you. Can't wait to get started," I mutter under my breath. Of all the arrogant, stubble-covered, mouth-breathing jocks I've ever met, Emmett York definitely takes the cake. I've met guys like him before, though. Guys who think they're God's gift to women, topped off by a healthy dose of overactive testosterone. What girl hasn't? My mom got derailed by men like that. I steer clear.

But this particular jerk is going to be my boss. Part of me considers thanking Ms. Raybourne and excusing myself from this entire process. Except I need a place to live, and the money is the answer to all of Mama Lily's problems. This is full-time work, better than any server job I could get, with better hours. Besides, Emmett York plays hockey. He'll travel, train, and do whatever else is involved with being a professional athlete. Stuff that will keep him away from me. Wasn't that why he was hiring me to care for his daughter? Because he wouldn't be around much?

Surely, this won't be that bad. We just got off to a rough start, that's all. It'll be fine.

"Did you say something, Ms. Harlow?" Ms. Raybourne stares hard at me.

"Nope," I finally say, gritting my teeth as I smile again. "I'm good."

"Great. And you agree to the arrangement?" she asks.

"Yes. I do." This job is the answer to my prayers. I plan to succeed at it, and I've never failed when I've set my mind to something.

"Great." She nods, then launches into the paperwork. The next half hour is a whirlwind of background checks, health insurance options, and tax forms. Finally, I head to the parking lot. The key fob on my old car doesn't work, so I unlock it manually and slide in. I drop the folder of information about Tabatha York on the passenger seat.

Tonight, I'm going to read through the file and get acquainted with my charge. I'll also need to brainstorm ways to take on Emmett York. We didn't get off to a great start, but a challenge has never stopped me. I like people, and being likable is a cornerstone to my personality. With some work and after a brief adjustment period, I'm sure this job is going to be just the right fit for me.

Duke

I KNOCK ON MY daughter's bedroom door. Again. "Tab, you need to open this." I'm met with silence, so I try again. "Don't you want me to tuck you in?" When there's still no response, I sigh and lean my forehead against the closed door. "Come on, baby. This is going to be fine."

"No, it isn't." My daughter's voice is barely audible through the door. "I don't want a nanny. I want Nana to watch me." Since I told Tabby I officially hired a nanny, she's been hiding in her room.

"You know why Nana can't watch you."

My mother-in-law broke her leg last month in Switzerland. She's in rehab there, and they expect a full recovery, but I don't know how long it'll be until she can keep up with an active seven-year-old.

The door opens so fast, I might have lost my balance if I wasn't a highly trained professional hockey player. Still, the quick movement makes my hamstrings scream. Stupid leg day.

Tabby stares up at me, a miniature version of myself. The same stubborn jaw and intense glare. At least half of her light brown hair has escaped from her ponytail, creating a cloud of flyaway chaos around her miserable face. "I promise, if Nana can watch me, I'll be the best girl in the whole world."

My stomach clenches. "Tabby, this has nothing to do with you not being a good girl."

"Then why are you doing this to me?" Her eyes swim with tears. She throws herself on her bed, burying her face in her elbow.

As always, I have no idea what to do when presented with tears, and that includes my daughter's. I pick my way through the sea of clothing and toys in her room with the same trepidation I might approach a tiger. Lowering myself on the bed next to her, I consider patting her on the back. But I'm sure it would be awkward for both of us, so I don't.

"We need help. Not because either of us is good or bad, but because we can't do everything that we have to do alone."

"We always have before." Her muffled voice is so small I can barely hear it.

She's not wrong. Since her mother died when she was a baby and it became only the two of us, we've managed ourselves. My mother-in-law would take care of Tabatha when I went out of town. On the few occasions she couldn't watch her, I asked either Shelly Taylor or Hillary Schwartz. Other times, I used the childcare service my team recommended. It didn't happen often, though. But between Sonya's mom's rehab and Tabby getting older, I decided this year we should hire someone to help us full time.

Tabby is painfully shy, and her shyness got worse toward the end of first grade, when she began to struggle in school. Her guidance counselor suggested a permanent caretaker versus a series of part-time help would be better in the long run. I hope that's not wrong.

I brace myself to deliver the arguments I've already made to her. "We had Nana before. And you weren't in school or gymnastics or ballet." The extracurricular activities were my mother-in-law's idea. She thought if Tabby could make some friends out of school, it would give her confidence in school. So far, all it's done is run me all over and stress out my daughter. "I met the nanny today. Her name's June."

Tabby peeks at me from under her folded elbow. "You did?"

I muster up as much enthusiasm as I can. "I did." She waits expectantly, so I wrack my brain for information that will be helpful. "She seems very... energetic." I resist the urge to press a palm to my forehead. Energetic? That's the best I can offer her?

It's not like I can tell her what my real first impressions were. Gorgeous creamy skin, covered in the prettiest layer of freckles I've ever seen. I've never thought I was a freckle guy, but they suit June Harlow. Average height, but legs seemed a lot longer than average. Graceful hands and red hair. Bright hazel eyes.

In the beginning of this process, the recruiter described her as "a human ray of sunshine." That sounded good, like perfect nanny material. Her education credentials are impeccable. As Raybourne pointed out, most of the other candidates didn't have college degrees, let alone dual certifications in education. Compared to the other applicants, June Harlow's list of referrals was also impressive. Countless people she babysits for and two different day care supervisors. Her bosses at the diner. A handful of neighbors from the foster home where she lived longest.

I don't know that many people who would vouch for me, so I called a few of June's references. I started with her day care supervisors. They only had the best things to say about her—that June is a natural with kids and gets along with everyone she meets. I learned she lived with Mama Lily, a retired librarian who took in as many foster kids as she could in her rambling house in the suburbs in New Jersey. I don't know where June was before that, but when she got to Mama Lily, she was a model student and neighbor. She helped with lawn work, carried in groceries, and watched people's pets. Mostly, she looked out for the younger kids.

A regular do-gooder.

When I connected with Mrs. Sharp, though, she convinced me June would be the right choice for Tabby. Apparently, June tutored her son, Matthew, last year. At eight, he struggled in school, couldn't focus, got frustrated easily. He fell behind. But after he started working with June, he improved. This year, his grades are up, and he's made friends. Most important to his mother, though, is that he regained his confidence.

His story sounds eerily close to Tabby's, and I want his outcome for her.

Right now, I stare at my daughter. She's never been confident. I used to worry it was because she was growing up without a mother, but when her grades plummeted last year at school, I wondered if there wasn't more to it. But between training and my game schedule, I can't keep a close enough eye on her. I need someone who can, someone who can help her. And June Harlow sounded like that kind of person.

Raybourne agreed. As the communications director, she liaisons between the players and public relations. It isn't her job to help me hire a nanny. But last year the team dealt with a hurricane of scandals and bad publicity. The last thing our team needs is negative press, so I wanted to be sure whoever I brought on passed Raybourne's impeccable judgment. After she met June, she stopped looking. She called me right away, yammering on about how this was the perfect fit. There was a list of glowing observations—optimistic, upbeat, open.

She wasn't wrong. The woman I met today appears to be all those things. Trusting eyes, laugh lines, and an easy smile. And if June Harlow can help my Tabby, then she's the right candidate for the job. I just need to forget the adorable dimple on her cheek and the way her eyes danced when she smiled. She's going to be my employee. I have no business noticing dancing eyes and cute dimples.

"I really think you're going to like her." I hope that's true. "With how much I need to travel, it'll make me feel better that you're here with someone you like and trust." All of that is true, but more important, I know if I make it about me, Tabby will be more likely to go along with the arrangement. Tabby is shy, but she's also fiercely protective of her loved ones. I'm not above leaning on that right now to coax my daughter to give this a chance—for both of us. "You know how important this year is going to be." I don't continue, but she nods. We both know I plan to retire at the end of the year. I'm almost thirty, and I have nearly constant back pain. This will be my last run, my last chance at a Stanley Cup. "I need to know you're safe."

"I know, Dad." She scoots to sit, folding her hands in her lap. Her voice sounds much too old to be coming from a seven-year-old. "You're right."

"I'm always right." I offer her an imperious look, the one that makes rookies quake in their skates. She giggles.

"Daddy." She rolls her eyes.

"It's time for bed, baby." I pat the bed, and she nods. As we move through her familiar bedtime routine, though, I hope for both of our sakes that I am actually right about our new nanny.

June

AT EXACTLY THREE O'CLOCK the next afternoon, I ring the doorbell to the York house, a stately colonial tucked away on a quiet street in Haddonfield, New Jersey. I don't know why, but I assumed the professional athletes all lived downtown in Philadelphia. One of my college friends dated a guy on the baseball team, and that's where the baseball players lived. It's the hippest place for young and wealthy singles, and I suppose that's what most of the young athletes are. Haddonfield is one of the older suburbs of Philadelphia. Lots of expensive but tasteful cars on the street. Plenty of manicured lawns. It reminds me of Lily's house in Moorestown, about fifteen minutes away, and it's exactly the kind of place people dream of raising their children. Well, it's the sort of place I hope to raise mine. Someday. Last night I discovered the Philadelphia Tyrants team practices in a facility in southern New Jersey, so I guess it's convenient. Just unexpected.

Then again, after yesterday's interaction with my new employer, I have no idea what to expect. Mentally, I rehearse what I plan to say. Remembering how he caught me investigating him brings a flush to my face. Not exactly my best first impression.

I square my shoulders. There's nothing I can do about that now, so no point in dwelling on it. We had a rough start, but we're going to be working together for months. I'll apologize. Get it out in the open so we can move on. He still hired me, after all. That must mean something.

I clutch a Tupperware container to my chest with one hand and grip my worn, taped-together suitcase with the other. I brought cookies for Tabatha. They're chocolate chip, a classic and one of my specialties. Mama Lily's own recipe, made with browned butter. According to the file they gave me yesterday, Tabby doesn't have any allergies, so I assume homemade baked goods will be okay. Besides, Lily always says sweets soften people up. With any luck, they'll work on Tabby's father, too.

The lock disengages, and the door swings open. I pin a smile on my lips.

If I was anxious before, a doorway full of Emmett York does nothing to calm me down. He's not the pretty kind of good-looking. In jeans and a T-shirt, bare feet, and covered in scruff, he's rugged, muscular, and moves with the sort of grace I expect from predators in the wild. Also, he has the hottest feet of anyone I've ever met. In fact, he's the definition of masculine hotness.

He also smells amazing.

I take a deep breath and launch into what I prepared to say. "Good afternoon, Mr. York. Before we get started, I want to apologize for yesterday. We got off on the wrong foot. I know nothing about hockey, and no one had given me the name of my new employer until I got to the second interview. Obviously, I was curious." The words are a rush of air, and I gesticulate along with them. "Since I like to be informed—"

"You decided to Internet stalk me?"

I'm sure one side of his mouth twitches. Is he laughing at me? I shrug. "Well, not in front of you. And I didn't plan to get caught." Of course I intended to Internet stalk him. Isn't that what everyone does when they need to know things about people? I inhale and motion to the door. Pasting a smile on my face, I try again. "May I come in?"

He steps to the side and waves me through. "By all means, Miss Harlow."

"June," I say as I step around him. "You should call me June. I am going to be living in your house, after all."

"Duke," he mutters.

"What?" I ask, lugging my suitcase in beside me.

"That's what people call me," he adds. "Duke. Because of my last name. Like the Duke of York."

"Right." I read that somewhere. In his foyer, I'm surprised again. He had updated all the spaces, even though the home appeared to be older, maybe even historic. There are gleaming hardwood floors underfoot and a sparkling chandelier overhead. I'm painfully aware of how my luggage and I don't fit here. I glance around. "Is Tabatha here? I've been looking forward to meeting her."

"It's Tabby. She hates Tabatha." He closes the door behind me, crossing his arms over his wide chest. "She'll be home from school in a few minutes." He motions to my luggage. "What's this?"

Isn't it obvious? "My clothes."

"Your clothes."

"Well, yeah." I shrug. "I have some winter clothes and jackets in storage. When it gets cold, I'll pick them up." I narrow my eyes. "This does offer room and board, correct? I mean, I plan to help with the cooking and housework, but I thought I would live here."

My stomach sinks. I don't want to call Ava back. "I'm sure that's what Ms. Raybourne—"

He stops me. "You don't need to help with housework."

"Of course, I'll help with housework."

"And it does come with room and board," he says like I hadn't even spoken. "I just expected more."

"More what?"

"Suitcases."

"More suitcases? I only have the one."

"You only have one suitcase? Or enough clothes for the one?"

"Both." The way he's looking at my suitcase makes me feel awkward. "I've never really seen the need for much stuff," I offer. "I feel like people waste a lot, and I prefer to live smaller. Plus, I just graduated from school, and there isn't much space in dorms, as you know—"

He lifts his hand to stop me. "Miss Harlow, has anyone told you that you talk a lot?"

Tough crowd. "Well, yeah. But not usually this soon after meeting me." When his brows only crinkle, I sigh. "I'm just nervous." I immediately feel the blush flood my cheeks and want to call back the words.

His eyebrows hiked up. "I make you nervous?"

"No." I blurt out. "Absolutely not. That's ridiculous." I wave my hand and roll my eyes, as if that's the craziest thing I've ever heard. "I spend lots of time with tall, super-fit famous athletes."

I wanted him to smile or chuckle, something to dispel the tension. But I'm not prepared for his bark of laughter, and I'm definitely not ready for the flare of heat that rushes through me. If broody Duke is sexy, smiling Duke is next-level hot.

Of course this guy makes me nervous. Everything about him feels too sharp. He's too tall, too big, and his gaze is too intense. It's not only that, though. I've been around good-looking men before, and I've never felt this... unsettled. But Emmett York is aloof and almost painfully direct. Plus, uncomfortable situations don't seem to bother him. That makes no sense to me. I'm all about harmony, which is why I usually have no problem reading people and understanding exactly how to put them at ease. This man doesn't appear like he is at ease anywhere, and he doesn't seem to care. I don't know how to manage him.

Like now. He continues to stand in the doorway, staring at me with amusement, but he says nothing. I made him laugh, so it's his turn to make this less weird. But he doesn't. I have no idea what to do with that, how to set this situation on a safe and comfortable course, and I'm out of my element. The whole feeling is unpleasant, and I'm kind of annoyed at him for it.

I doubt being irritable with my new employer is the right play, though. Not if I want to keep this job, and I do. After reading through Tabby's file last night, I feel like I already know the little girl, and I feel like she needs me.

I change the subject. "Does Tabby know I'm coming?" She's seven, and usually girls that age are excited to meet people. Her chart mentioned that she's shy, but I assumed curiosity would get the best of her.

He nods, and the sides of his lips turn down. "I should warn you. Tabby has a hard time with new people. It's why I wanted to wait until we chose the right person to introduce them. Don't push her. It might take her a while to warm up to you." He crosses his arms over his enormous chest, glowering.

Did something in my resume give him the idea I would be a jerk to his daughter? "Okay."

"The bus drops her off right in front of the house. I usually watch from the porch. It's getting close." Shifting, he stares out the window next to the door, his brow creasing like he's afraid he missed it. In that moment, his guard slips, and the concern and anticipation there—to see his daughter—makes him look like a completely different person. With that softness on his face, he's more approachable and infinitely more good-looking. Not at all like an egotistical jerk.

Two things become painfully clear to me. First, though my employer unsettles me, he loves his daughter very much. Second, and decidedly more dangerous, is that Duke York is fascinating. One moment, he comes off frustratingly arrogant and the next, his face softens while he worries about his daughter. Add in the way my body reacts when he's close, and I need to be very careful with him.

I wasn't lying when I told Ms. Raybourne I wasn't interested in relationships, physical or otherwise. Yes, Lily needs me right now, but that's not all of it. I don't date much. I've been busy with school and work. When I have agreed to go out with someone, I stay away from men like Duke York. I prefer low-maintenance men—men who are easy to be with and easy enough to be without. I can't remember much of my mother, certainly not much good. But I remember the men she preferred, the fights and the drama, the euphoria and the sorrow. From early on, I decided I would steer clear of anything complex like that. It just caused pain for everyone.

Whatever Duke York is, it's complicated, and that's before I add in that he's my boss. He makes me want to growl at him one second, and then he makes my belly warm the next. That can't be good for a body at all. Right now, I need to stay focused on what it is I'm here to do. A little girl needs me.

"I'll just wait outside for Tabby." I hold out the Tupperware of cookies. "Could you put these in the kitchen, please? I baked them for you both." He only stares at my outstretched peace offering. When he doesn't reach for the cookies, I push them against him, forcing him to take them from me. "Right. Well, then." I motion toward the door, the manners Lily drummed into my head surfacing. "Did you want to join me?"

He shakes his head, as if waking from a dream. "No. I'll let you."

When he says nothing else, I back away toward the door. "Right. Well, great then." Unable to stand any more tension, I quickly step onto the porch. Pulling the door closed behind me, I exhale and roll my eyes. As I trudge down the driveway, I try to imagine any way that could have gone worse. Talking with him is painful.

A yellow school bus turns the corner. I hurry forward. I have a new friend to meet.

Duke

I can't help it. I watch June go to meet my daughter.

Though I wanted to go with her to the bus stop, to run interference for Tabby, I held myself back. It won't show Tabby I trust June if I hover. But I can't keep myself from watching through the window.

While June walks down the driveway, I realize I'm still holding the Tupperware container full of cookies. I open the lid, and the scent of warm brown sugar wafts to my nose. Unable to stop myself, I snag one, biting into it. It's the perfect cookie—chewy throughout—and the chocolate is still warm, like she pulled them out of the oven right before she came over. I try to keep my eyes from rolling back in my head. It's probably been years since I've had a homemade cookie this good. The only cookies I can manage are the kind from the log of dough I buy at the grocery store. I force myself to close the lid before I can eat a second one.

Outside, the bus stops in front of my house. Tabby hops down, but she barely gets onto the sidewalk before she freezes. It takes everything in me to stay still when my daughter looks so anxious. But I need to give June a chance.

As June kneels beside Tabby, I can't help but notice the fine curve of her face, the tilt of her chin. She's a beauty, that's for sure. She smiles at Tabby, talking the whole time, and Tabby nods along. But when June offers her a hand, my daughter steps away, her face conflicted. Her uncertainty stabs at my gut, but I continue watching, and that's the only reason I notice June's reaction.

When someone scoffs at a friendly overture, I expect them to look disappointed, hurt even. Maybe upset or irritated. I'm a short distance away, but I don't see any of that on June's face. Instead, she only looks accepting, as if my daughter's reaction is exactly what she expected. I don't understand that.

It's only a fleeting look, gone in a flash. Then her smile returns. Her mouth moves the entire walk up the drive while Tabby stares at the concrete in front of her. June Harlow definitely knows how to talk.

The two of them head for the house, and I abruptly step away from the window, not wanting to get caught staring. My gaze falls on the beat-up suitcase propped against the wall.

She had to be kidding. There's no way that's all of her things. No one is that much of a minimalist.

The door squeaks open, and they both step inside, letting in a wave of humidity. It's early summer in New Jersey. It's much hotter here at the beginning of the school year than I ever remembered in Toronto, where I grew up.

When Tabby sees me, she hurries forward, wrapping her arms around me. I tuck her against me. "Hey, Tabby Cat. How was your day at school?" I ask, glancing down at her. Her eyes stay on June, though, when she shrugs. Awkward tension descends on us, and I hate it. But I don't know how to get rid of it either. I've never been good with that kind of stuff, and I've certainly never experienced it around my daughter.

I don't like this, so I glare at June. In response, she smiles at us. "Tabby just agreed she would help me find a space for all my things." She motions to her suitcase. "Could you show me my room so I can get settled?"

Right now, I don't want to. Bringing in a stranger was a bad idea. I don't care what the guidance counselor or the team psychologist I consulted said. Tabby is right—we've always managed on our own.

But even as my instincts are to pull my daughter behind me, to hide her from this situation and her own discomfort, I force myself to do things differently. I peel Tabby from my side, but I keep hold of her hand. With the other, I grip the suitcase handle. "Come on, Tab. Let's show her the spare bedroom."

"Dad..." Tabby's voice is a whisper. She shakes her head. It's obvious she doesn't want to show June anywhere, that she doesn't want her in our house, and she wants to go hide somewhere.

I grit my teeth. "Come on." I squeeze her hand reassuringly, and we head upstairs together.

The house has seven bedrooms. When Sonya and I bought it nine years ago, right after I signed to the Tyrants, I hoped we would fill it with children. But then, two years later, she was gone, and it was only Tabby and me.

The room I planned for June is at the end of the hall, next to mine. It's the largest spare room and has its own en suite. I figured she would be more comfortable with her own bathroom. I deposit her battered luggage in the center of the room. Behind me, I hear a sharp inhale.

"It's lovely," she whispers. The way she's looking around the room is like I transported her to some other world. I follow her gaze. Objectively, the room is pretty. I hired someone to decorate after Sonya passed because Sonya didn't get far with her renovation plans. As always, she had grand ideas but fumbled with the follow-through.

June spins around in the center, her arms outstretched. "This room is big enough for four girls. Maybe six."

Uncomfortable, I wheel her suitcase into the center of the room. It's awkward, though, thanks to a broken wheel. "I'm glad you find it satisfactory." I've been called aloof before, but I'm not sure I've ever sounded so stuffy. Resisting the urge to roll my eyes, I sigh. "We'll leave you to get settled, then."

"Wait. Tabby agreed to help me." June smiles at my daughter, who looks miserable in response. "I'll never know where to put all my things in here."

"I'm sure you'll be able to figure it out," I add. Because it is very clear that my daughter wants nothing to do with June right now. If anything, she looks like she wants to escape. "Why don't we leave you to it?"

June shoots me a scowl and shakes her head. "Please?" She kneels down in front of Tabby. "I could use the company."

I know my daughter, and no matter how uncomfortable she might be, she won't be able to resist that. She steps forward and nods before gazing up at me. "It's okay, Daddy."

Swallowing hard, I back out of the room. "Right. Then I'll leave you two to it." But I don't close the door. I force myself to walk away, down the hall to my office. Once inside, I can't sit down. Pacing, I shake out my hands.

I hate seeing Tabby uncomfortable, and all my instincts tell me to shield her, to make this go away. When I lost her mom, I decided I would always do whatever was best for Tabby. But what would make us feel better and what's best for her are different things. Right now, she needs help, and by all measurable parameters, June's the right person for the job.

June, whose cheeky comebacks amuse me and whose cheerful smile makes me want to step closer, to bask in her happiness.

While June might be exactly what Tabby needs, I need to steer clear of her as much as I can. But that doesn't mean I can't make sure she's as prepared to care for Tabby as I can make her. It doesn't mean I can't make sure that Tabby has everything she needs.

I round my desk and pull out a pad of paper and a pen. Then I get to work.

June commandeers Tabby for almost an hour in her room. I busy myself with laundry. Our housekeeper, Mrs. Reyes, does most of the laundry, but I have nothing pressing tonight with the start of training camp tomorrow. Add in the preseason nerves, and I need to keep busy.

After I do some laundry, I hear them move into Tabby's room. Tabby doesn't say much, but I hear June cooing over Tabby's things. I linger upstairs, finding reasons to walk by the room so I can peek at them. When I can't figure out anything else to do upstairs, I decide to order dinner. I stop at the door and ask June if she likes pizza.

"Yes," she answers, lifting her head from a stack of Tabby's painting. "Thank you," she says, but her gritted teeth ruin the sentiment. I scowl back before I head downstairs, leaving them in the upstairs playroom.

I place the order and retreat to my downstairs office to watch film. After the pizza arrives, dinner is quiet. I try to talk to Tabby about school, but she clams up as usual. She gobbles down a slice and a half of pizza and then asks to be excused. I nod, and she scurries into the living room. The drone of the television follows her.

June and I eat the rest of our pizza in silence, seated across from each other at the island in my kitchen. She shifts in her seat. Finally, she asks, "So, how long have you lived here?" Her brown eyes are wide, genuinely curious.

"Nine years." I motion to her plate. "Finished?"

She nods. "Nine years. You must have been really young when you bought it, right?"

"Yes. Twenty." That had been a big year. After my rookie year with the Tyrants, management extended my contract, made me a franchise player. I met Sonya, a recent graduate from Penn, down at the shore. By the end of summer, I was married, had bought the house I assumed we would raise our family in, and planned to retire in Philadelphia. I marvel at twenty-year-old Emmett York's idyllic visions. "Listen, June—"

"That's how you start unpleasant conversations." She folds her napkin and flattens it under her fingers on the counter. "Terminal illness, breakups..."

I continue as she trails off. "We don't need to be friends."

Her head tilts. "Or just unpleasant declarations, I guess." She sighs. "I am aware we don't need to be friends, Duke. I just figured it might be nicer. Since I'm living under your roof."

Once again, I squash a pang of guilt. She hides it well, but I can tell she's offended. But guilt is easier than the alternative—actually doing as she suggests. Being friends with June feels dangerous. "I believe you're a good fit for Tabby, but it remains to be seen."

Her eyes widen and then narrow. When she speaks, though, it's carefully measured. "What we need is a little space. I only ask that you give us that. Unless you consider hovering and walking past the rooms that we're in a zillion times space." It's teasing, but I don't smile.

My hands fall to my hips. "I worry about my daughter. She's struggling."

"I get that, but you wouldn't have hired me if you didn't need help." She presses her lips together, and her eyes soften. I don't want to see compassion right now, though.

I glare at her. "It's just... you make me uncomfortable."

She jolts as if I slapped her. "What?"

Again, the flare of conscience. I ignore it, crossing my hands over my chest. "You're so cheerful. It's unnerving."

She pushes to stand. "That is the most ridiculous thing I've ever heard."

I agree—I sound like an idiot. But I don't want to admit how fascinating I find her or tell her that her smile feels more addicting than crack. The less time I spend with her, the safer for me. Except that makes me feel like a coward, and I hate that even more. I throw up my hands. "Can't you see this is awkward? It's obvious we don't get along."

She flinches, and it's decided—I'm a grade-A asshole. The pain on her face makes me feel small, and I swipe a hand over my hair, wondering if the floor could swallow me up. Her face smooths over instead. "Isn't that what you wanted? For us to not 'get along'? Everyone was worried I'd try to seduce you or something." Her cheeks redden at the word seduce, and again it frustrates me how I find her flushes so appealing. "At least you can be sure that won't happen."

"That's good news."

Her chin hitches up, and I haven't hated myself this much in a long time. Unable to look at her any longer, I pick up the papers I brought from my office earlier. "Training camp starts tomorrow, and I won't be around much. I want you to be prepared." I hand her the paperwork. "This is a list of emergency contact numbers. All my numbers, my email, Tabby's grandmother's number."

"The one who broke her leg?" she asks, and I nod. "Didn't you say she was in Switzerland?"

"Just in case you have questions and can't reach me."

"Right."

"I wrote up a detailed schedule of Tabby's activities. I've already contacted all of her teachers, her coaches, her guidance counselors... anyone you might need. They received the email and cell phone number you provided on your resume. Is that correct?" I wait for her nod before I retrieve my phone from my pocket. "I've got you programmed into my phone as well."

She scans the papers I handed her. "Did you really write 911 next to the emergency number?"

I ignore her. "Tab has a dance class tomorrow at three. I'll text you the directions. There's a car in the garage you can use to drive her." I'll drive the convertible so she can use the Range Rover. The two-seat BMW is fine unless the weather is bad. It doesn't handle well in the snow.

"I'd prefer to take my car."

"The car on the street?" I shake my head. "Absolutely not. You shouldn't even be driving that thing." Her car is probably older than she is, and I'm not even sure what color it originally was.

She glares at me, but when she speaks, it's clear she's trying to be professional. "I just took it in for a tune-up."

"That thing couldn't carry a tune if you strapped one to the roof rack."

Her brow furrows in confusion. "It doesn't have a roof rack."

I finish setting our dinner dishes in the sink. "I'll leave my car."

She sighs. "How far away is her dance studio?"

"It's only in town. A mile or so."

"You know, we could walk in an emergency."

"I would prefer that you didn't have to."

She folds her arms over her chest. "Aren't you going to be at the practice facility? That's only a couple of miles away. I could call you if we have any problems."

"I'll be in camp."

Her mouth tightens. It's clear she's trying to stay reasonable. I'm not sure why she's bothering—I don't sound reasonable at all. "Then I could call the facility, and they would go get you."

I don't feel like arguing anymore, but there's no reason for Tabby to be in that questionable car when I have a different, perfectly acceptable alternative. "Consider it a perk of the job. And I'd like you to keep me posted about everything. How she's feeling, what she's done, your thoughts and observations. Everything." I pull my wallet out of my pocket. "Here's my credit card."

"You're giving me your credit card?" She sounds surprised. That makes sense since I've acted like a jackass.

I soften my tone. "You can charge anything she needs. Food, clothes, whatever. Just let me know, okay?" Having said everything I needed to say, I head toward the living room to join Tabby. At the doorway, though, I pause, unable to leave it like this. When I look back, she's still standing, staring at the papers I gave her. "For what it's worth, June, I still think you're the right choice for Tabby."

She offers me a stiff nod, and I escape, joining my daughter on the couch. June doesn't join us, but I don't expect her to. I wouldn't want to be with me right now if I was her, either.

It's for the best. Setting the precedent early will help us long-term. Maybe by then I'll get used to feeling like a dick.

June

I'm glad Duke's gone by the time I wake up the next morning. It saves me from any more awkward conversations before I've had coffee. The only evidence he had been there was a rinsed-out mug in the dishwasher.

Last night's conversation was eye-opening. I lay in bed for a long time, playing it over in my head. Any residual hope we could have a normal, adult-like working relationship died. I wish it didn't bother me, but it does. I've spent my entire life trying to be likable, and for him to write me off before he even gives me a chance... it makes me feel helpless in a way I don't understand.

Admittedly, we didn't get off on the right foot, but I did everything I could to patch that up. It's clear he has no intention of smoothing things over with me. In his mind, I'm his daughter's nanny. Apparently, that job position doesn't require even the most basic friendly interactions.

One thing is certain—Duke needs me as much as his daughter does. The two of them are closed off, quiet and unreadable, even around each other. But when he was telling me about his worries, how he's not sure if I'm right for Tabby, I couldn't help but notice he looked desperate. He might hate watching his daughter struggle, but I can't help thinking he doesn't know how to fix the problem either.

I've rallied today. I still have a job, and I still believe I can do some good for Tabby. Maybe I can even help her stubborn father, too.

After a quick shower, I start the morning routine Duke has meticulously mapped out for us. When I walk into Tabby's room, she grumbles when I wake her up. Maybe it's me. I've always been a morning person, and my experience with non-morning people is they find us annoying. But after some coaxing, she's vertical and dressed for school.

I can't find much food in the house, so I scramble some eggs. Tabby eats them grudgingly, offering only the shortest answers to questions. When she finishes, she brushes her teeth, and I do my best to tame her tangled blond hair into a ponytail. The brush she has isn't the best for detangling, so I make a note to buy something better. It's bad enough to brush knots out of long hair. The proper tools help.

I prod her out the door just in time for the bus, reminding myself to give her more time tomorrow. Sloths move faster than Morning Tabby.

But as I walk her to the bus stop, I notice offhand that I don't see my car. The bus rounds the corner, and I wave goodbye to her. As it pulls away, I glance down the street. I still don't see my car anywhere. There's no way I forgot where I parked. I'd been so nervous when I pulled up, and I was afraid I would park in front of a fire hydrant.

After a walk back and forth, it's clear my car isn't there. I hurry back to the house, throwing open the front door. I'm sure I left my keys on the foyer table. There had been another set there, and I assumed they were Duke's. The basket there is empty now, though.

I need to call someone. Or I'll text Duke. Maybe he knows. Maybe there's some tow-away zone I didn't notice. I left my phone in the kitchen, and when I snag it, I see an envelope on the counter. I didn't notice it when I was making breakfast. My name's spelled out in tidy block letters on the front. Sliding a finger under the flap, I unseal it. A key falls out along with a slip of paper.

The Range Rover is in the garage if you need it.
D

What the hell does that mean? I turn the key in my palm and head for the garage, as if it's the missing piece of a puzzle. Sure enough, I find a gleaming white Range Rover parked in the third stall in the massive garage. I press the unlock button on the key in my hand, and the SUV beeps, confirming the key will work. Did I think it wouldn't? Honestly, I have no idea what I should think. I told Duke last night I wanted to use my car. But this morning, my car is gone, and he's left me the keys to his like he didn't even hear me last night.

Why would that surprise me? Duke doesn't strike me as someone who cares if others disagree with him.

Locking the car, I go back inside, seething. How dare he do something with my car without asking me? I might be his employee, but that's my personal property.

Snagging my phone off the counter, I hurry upstairs to my beautiful room. I still can't believe it's all for me. Even the towels I used after my shower this morning are the nicest I've ever used. Ten-year-old me—the girl who always had to share a bedroom with at least two other people—wouldn't know what to do with herself in this room. Grown-up me hardly does either. I'm almost afraid to touch anything, worried I'll break something or that the whole place will go up in smoke, like some sort of dream.

I squash the joy this lovely space brings me as I sift through the stack of papers Duke handed me last night, searching for the contacts list.

Opening my messages, I type in his number. I pause, trying to think of a diplomatic way to ask my question. I settle for: *Good morning. Where is my car?*

An immediate response. *This phone is set to Do Not Disturb. I'll respond when I see your message.*

I seethe. He stole my car, and he's not even accepting messages? I put my hands on my hips and pace back and forth in my room. I planned to check on Lily today. It's been a couple of days since I went to the assisted-living facility, and I worry they aren't taking good enough care of her.

I guess I'm taking the Range Rover if I want to go anywhere. Sifting through the paperwork Duke gave me, I scan his schedule. A plan forms. Ripping into him won't help me keep this job, even though I feel it's my right. Who takes someone's car without asking? Duke York, apparently. Maybe he hopes I'll get angry, go off on him. That would give him a reason to get rid of me, and something tells me a part of him would like that. He might know he needs help, but he's not happy about it.

Well, I'm not about to give him that option. He wants to be an overbearing jerk? Fine. But Lily always said you catch more flies with honey than vinegar.

Duke

THE FIRST DAY OF training camp is a disaster. Half our veterans huffed and puffed through it. These guys don't seem to have done any cardio this summer beyond getting off the couch for a beer and sitting back down. The new guys—and there are a lot of them—are in better shape. They need to be. If they want to differentiate themselves as rookies, they need to come in as prepared as possible. Most of our young guys are on one-year contracts. They don't have the time to slack off.

I call the entire group together in the meeting room before lunch. The coaches make themselves scarce.

Last year was a fiasco. We struggled from the start, plagued by bad morale, thanks to a few overpaid and entitled prima donnas. When Brandon McPhee, an up-and-coming center, started talking to the press about the locker-room infighting, most of which he caused, things deteriorated. Coach Hargreeves backed me at the end of the season, going to bat with the organization and management. At the end, I was the last man standing. During free agency, our team traded five of our veteran high-profile players, including McPhee, and replaced them with young, upcoming prospects. I could tell from management spending that they are rebuilding for the future, and my guess is they don't have high hopes for a playoff run this year.

But I do. These guys will be here in the years to come, but I won't. This is my time.

We're in for an uphill battle. As I stare at my team, I try to come up with something inspiring. Except I'm not much of an orator. So, I drop my hands on my hips and lean in on my strengths—honesty and straight shooting.

I inhale, let my gaze pause on each of the guys in front of me, and I say, "Today was a fucking shit show."

At one end of the room, Colt Carmichael snorts before he covers his mouth. This is his fourth year on the team, so he's used to my pep talks. Besides, he doesn't have much to worry about. Of all my veterans, he and his roommate, Rocco Barnett, are the most prepared. They're good guys, serious about their careers. They might partake in the nightlife downtown, and I've heard rumors about their exploits with the ladies. But they show up, work hard, and keep their fucking traps shut. So, I ignore him, but stare down Charlie Haskins and Finn Kennedy. Last year, the two defensemen mostly stayed out of the team drama, and management didn't target them for trades. But they certainly haven't proved that they deserve to still be here yet.

"Seems like a bunch of you spent more time on the beach sipping margaritas when you should have been in the gym." I get a few dirty looks, but they're from guys who deserve my ire. To make sure the young guys who came in prepared don't think I'm pissed at them, I catch a few gazes and soften my tone. "Those of you who took their off-season seriously, kudos. Mason," I call out to Hunter Mason, a promising recent sign from Chesterboro University who got an invitation to training camp, "and Lancaster"—I point to Travis

Lancaster, a defenseman we just called up from the minors—"you both particularly impressed me. Keep it up."

I sigh. Starting the season by ripping them a new one probably isn't setting the right tone, so I search for something better. Again, I opt for honesty. "Last year was a mess. Our team spent more time scoring space on sports gossip columns than scoring goals, and we ended with the worst record in the eastern conference. This is a new year, and we're a new group. We get to decide how we move forward from here. I don't want to spend another year caught up in all that shit. Let's show our fans and ourselves we have what it takes to make a run for the Cup." That's met with some clapping and a few hoots.

"Starting tomorrow, I'll be leading runs." There are a few groans, but no one has the balls to do it loud enough to attract my direct attention. "Every morning. We'll meet here before practice. Gentlemen, we have a month until our season opener. Until that time, you need to live, breathe, and eat hockey. No distractions. We need your complete focus. That starts at six tomorrow morning, assholes. I'll see you all here then." I motion around the room. "Check the board before you leave. There is a list of meetings."

I adjourn my pep talk, and my teammates stand, gather their things, and chat for a few before they head out. I toss my personal stuff in my bag and check my phone. There are two texts from June earlier today asking about her car.

Frowning, I pull up a new message and text my mechanic. I had him pick her car up this morning. Last night, when June was talking about driving Tabby around, it made me anxious. I don't even like Tabby's grandmother driving her, and Nancy's car is only a couple years old. If June is going to insist on using her own car, I want to make sure it's in good shape. I told Mike, my mechanic, to run it through its paces, check tires, brakes, the works. I hoped he would have it back before she noticed it was missing.

I guess I was wrong.

I glance through the window next to the door. As if on cue, June Harlow appears, and Tabby's wandering beside her, licking an ice cream cone. Today, June's wearing a flowing red skirt and a sleeveless white blouse with flip-flops. It's hot, so she pulled her long red hair up in a messy bun on top of her head. Even from here, I can tell she's not wearing any makeup. Every single freckle is on display.

That's right—I gave her my normal camp schedule. That would tell her conditioning is over, and we have an hour's break. I'm still surprised to see her, though.

A low whistle draws my attention back to my teammates. "Who's that?" Rocco Barnett leans forward, staring out the window. He must have noticed my distraction.

I glare at him. "Tabby's nanny. Hands off." I hold his eyes until he shows me his palms.

"Got it, Duke. Off-limits." He winks at me. "She's all yours."

I cross my arms over my chest and scowl. "She's not mine. I mean, she's my nanny. Or Tabby's nanny." I inhale, regroup. "She's my employee. Which means you all need to treat her with complete respect." I don't know the dating habits of the new guys, so I focus my irritation on Barnett and Colt Carmichael, my two known playboys. Colt chuckles, and Rocco tosses me a salute.

They head for the locker room door, still obviously amused by me. I glare at them. As I push through the door to calm down my new nanny, she makes eye contact. Her face splits into a bright grin. It takes almost superhuman power to ignore the way her smiles heat me up.

I need to take my own advice.
Hands off.

June

Duke's still wearing workout clothes. His hair is wet, falling in wavy tendrils around his face. Yesterday, I objectively considered him the best-looking man I'd ever met, when he was telling me we didn't have to be friends, but today, covered in sweaty man muscles? He's the hottest thing I've ever seen, men in movies and magazines included.

As he approaches me, I struggle to recall everything I planned to say to him. When he stops in front of me, all six feet a couple inches of just-worked-out flesh, I need to shake my head to clear it. Scrambling to recover, I paste a smile on my face. "Tabby wanted to see you. For your first day of camp."

Next to me, Tabby stops licking her ice cream. "Nuh uh. You wanted ice cream."

Traitor. "I did. And we brought you some yogurt. Tabby said you don't eat ice cream during the season." I hold out the to-go container to him.

He stares at it like it's a snake. Or more like it could be a Trojan horse. His eyes narrow. "You brought me ice cream?"

"Yogurt." I point to it. "And we drove it here in the Range Rover." I lift my eyebrows. "Because I think someone stole my car."

He folds his arms over his chest, and his forehead furrows. "No one in their right mind would steal that car."

I grimace. *Fair point.* Reaching into my pocket, I pull out a handful of quarters. "Tabby, you said you wanted to check out the arcade, right?" When I brought up that we could visit her father at the rink, Tabby didn't want to go at first, but then she mentioned the rink had some video games, and I could coax her.

Now, she swipes the coins from my hand and scurries off. The arcade is within eyesight, and the rink is closed for camp, so she's safe there. When she's out of hearing range, I hold out the yogurt, and he takes it from me. I try again. "Duke, could you tell me what happened to my car?"

"I asked my mechanic to look it over."

I'm not sure what I expected when I came to visit him at the practice facility. Part of me wondered if he would say anything about taking my car if I didn't somehow confront him about it. But I didn't expect this.

A mechanic? My brain tallies the cost of my car's potential repairs. The number it spits out makes me nauseous.

"I see." I inhale and do my best to plan the most diplomatic response I can. "You do realize that is my personal property. I would have appreciated it if you had cleared that with me." If he had, I would have told him I don't have money for a mechanic.

He exhales, and for the first time, I realize he looks tired. My alarm went off at six o'clock, and he was already gone, so I have no idea what time he woke up this morning. Add that to the sporty, fitness things he probably did all day, and he has a right to his exhaustion. I get tired just putting on my shoes sometimes.

"I should have sent you a message this morning when I contacted Mike."

"Mike?"

"My mechanic." He runs a hand through his disheveled hair, but it falls back exactly how it was. "I texted him this morning to see if he could give your car some TLC."

"I told you I just had it tuned up." *Three months ago,* I add in my head. I don't want to admit he's right. My car probably needs an oil change, maybe a bunch of other things too. But they're things I can't afford without a paycheck. They need to wait.

"You said." He cocks his head, as if he'll allow that fact in the debate. I want to roll my eyes at his arrogance. "And I told you there was a better option than your car in my garage. Then last night I realized you might not be comfortable driving the big SUV. So, I reached out to Mike to make sure your car was as safe as possible before you started driving Tabby around." When I glance away, taking in the lobby at the practice facility, he continues. "I don't even like Tabby riding with my mother-in-law, and her car is brand new. Please, just give me this. If you don't like the big SUV, I can get us a smaller car for you."

I shift my weight. This morning, I'd been furious. I couldn't imagine what explanation he would have to take my car with no warning. But this... I can't blame him for looking out for his daughter. And he was worried I might be nervous driving the SUV? If anything, all of this is almost endearing. Is it possible to be endearing and overbearing at the same time? Somehow, he seems to manage it.

But he talks about buying another car like it's a thing people do with no real thought or anxiety. My life has never had financial stability. What must it be like to not worry about things like that?

What would it be like if I could get my car fixed without being concerned that I wouldn't have the money to pay my bills for the rest of the month?

Finally, I sigh and admit, "It's just... I don't have the money for any automotive work right now."

He blinks at me. "I called Mike. My mechanic, my treat."

I shake my head. "But it's my car. It's not your responsibility to pay for it." He opens his mouth to argue further, and I rush forward. "This is... really generous." That doesn't feel right, but it isn't wrong either. "But I'm not a charity case." The words resurface memories I pretend don't exist, and they give away more about me than I wanted to.

I resulted from a teenage pregnancy, and my mother never hid the fact I was an unwelcome accident. I grew up with constant reminders I shouldn't have been born. When she turned me over to foster care, I had a backpack of personal items and the clothes on my back. My wardrobe has always consisted of hand-me-downs, and I have always been asked to find a place for myself within a space that always felt crowded. One more kid in a room, one more mouth to feed. A life of constant imposition.

I'm an adult now. I want to make my own way.

Duke searches my face, and I have no idea what he finds there. I tilt my chin up.

"You're my employee," he offers, as if testing the waters on this approach. I nod because it's a factual statement. "And... if I want to give you a bonus to pay for your car—a car you'll be driving my daughter around in—then I can do that, can't I?" When I huff out an exhale and try to find another argument, he hurries on. "He was supposed to have it back before you had to get Tabby to dance later.

But I have no problem with you using the Range Rover as long as you want. Whenever you want."

"That car probably cost more than my college education." I drove under the speed limit the entire ride here.

"So?" He shrugs. "It's only a car."

I can only blink. Only a car? I can't process the differences in our perspective.

"It's a big car, which is why I bought it," he continues. "Makes it safe in an accident."

"I will not get in any accidents." I have a spotless driving record.

"I didn't say you would." He enunciates each word clearly. "But there are other people on the road. My job is to keep you and Tabby as safe as I can make you."

I can't think of any response to that. In fact, all the words have evacuated my brain. In my entire life, I don't think anyone has ever worried about my safety. Not like this.

It's... nice. Unexpected and really nice.

He lifts his hands. "Your car should be back in the driveway in a couple of hours."

It's not an apology, but it's as close as I expect I'll get from him. I continue to study him, but it's like the pieces don't fit. One moment, he's being overbearing, almost rude, and the next he does something like this? No one has ever given me this big of a gift before. I understand that it's for his daughter's benefit as well. But it's my car he's had fixed. Finally, I say, "I thought you didn't like me."

He blinks in surprise. "I never said I didn't like you."

"All that stuff about us not getting along? How I'm too cheerful and I make everything awkward?" Even repeating the words hurts my feelings. "That we can't be friends?"

He pauses, his eyes wide. "That doesn't mean I don't like you."

I stare at him. That makes no sense. But we're at his workplace, and this conversation has gotten more personal than I expected. I only planned to come to show him he wouldn't scare me away. This has become something different.

I take a couple of steps back. "Okay, then. I'll just wait for my car. Back at the house." Searching for something to lighten the mood, I motion to his yogurt. "We got you pineapple. Tabby said it's your favorite."

"Thank you. It is."

"Right." I swallow. "And thank you. For my car."

"No problem." He swipes his hand over his hair once more before he heads back to the locker room.

I watch him go. The more conversations I have with Duke York, the less I feel like I understand him at all.

Duke

I MANAGE A SHOWER and then head for the room where the team dietician has set up lunch. From here on, I'll be on dietary restrictions. During the season, when I'm not eating at the rink, I have a food service prepare meals for Tabby and me. But I don't need to worry about that here. On training days, the team will feed us. Now, I fill up a plate—heavy on protein, fat, and complex fiber—and take a seat at an empty four-person table.

I put the yogurt June brought me next to my plate. I still can't believe she brought me the treat despite being irritated about the car. As I shovel food into my face, I check my phone repeatedly. I don't expect any texts from June, but I can't be sure of her. Our conversations leave me off-kilter. I can't seem to say the right things. My phone stays silent, though.

Our goalie, Huck Sokolov, sits down beside me, plopping his plate of food in front of him. He motions to the phone. "Did our captain's text get left on read?"

I pick it up and slide it into my pocket. "Just making sure Tabby's nanny doesn't need anything else."

"The nanny, huh?" He keeps his voice low so only the two of us can hear. He whistles under his breath. "Is that who she was? She's cute."

"Shut up, Huck." I keep my eye on my food.

"Good comeback." He chuckles. "But I saw you guys talking. No distractions, you say? Tell me more about that."

I glance up and meet his amused gaze. "What does that mean?"

He rolls his eyes. "Please. We've been playing together too long for you to pull that on me." His slight Russian accent comes out toward the end of the sentence, but as always, it's so faint most people probably wouldn't even notice it. That's by design. Huck moved to the States to play in his early teens. He's been trying to get rid of his accent since then.

"I'm serious. She's taking care of my daughter."

"So?"

"So... it would be really stupid to start something with someone who works for me. Especially someone who lives under the same roof as my daughter." I run a hand over my beard. It's reached the itchy phase. "Besides, you know me better than that. All my attention is on the season ahead."

His face becomes serious. "Good. Because I need you at your best this year." He motions around the room. "Most of these guys have years ahead of them to make a run for the Cup. But the two of us?" He moves his hand between us. "This might be the end for us. Let's not take any chances."

I glare at him, and he stares back. But we've both been around for a long time. Male posturing doesn't intimidate either of us. What's more is that I don't have an excuse for him. I haven't announced my retirement, but I'm sure a bunch of the guys suspect. Back pain and injuries have plagued me for the last few years. My time is running out. And Huck? His reaction time is slower. Not much slower, but at our performance level, every split second matters.

What's more is he's right—I have been distracted by June today. I want to think I've been worrying about Tabby, but that's not it. I keep thinking about how she looked eating pizza last night, in her sweats and worn T-shirt with Rutgers stretched across it, her red hair in a haphazard heap on top of her head and every freckle in stark contrast on her face. That's not where my attention should be. There's no way I can harp on the guys about staying focused and avoiding distractions when I'm not doing the same.

So, I nod at Huck, and he nods back. In agreement, he slaps me on the shoulder and walks away without another word.

Huck is right, but so is June. Tabby needs someone to be there for her, someone who can help with her schoolwork, and June's the right person for the job. It isn't her fault I find everything about her too appealing. That's my problem, and I won't let my issues interfere with what Tabby needs.

I need to hold my shit together. Nothing can happen between the two of us, but that doesn't mean we can't be friends, like she suggested. Granted, I don't have many good friends and no women friends to speak of. But Tabby is so young, and right after Sonya died, I didn't have the emotional capacity to do much more than play hockey and be a single dad. When I finally came out of the first dark days, it was easier to keep it that way. Between my teammates and raising my young daughter, it left little time for hanging out with the boys or dating.

Did I miss that stuff? Sometimes. Tabby is my world, though. It was a small price to pay.

Still, June could have a point. Friendship between us would be better for Tabby. If this is going to be successful, we need to figure out a working partnership—and I need to find a way to be friendly and keep my hands to myself.

I open the lid on the Styrofoam container of yogurt, and I do my best not to think about the woman who brought it for me.

June

AFTER WE LEAVE THE practice facility, I take Tabby grocery shopping with me. Last night, Duke ordered in. He mentioned he has a food service he uses during the season, but that doesn't sound that healthy. It's probably one of those fancy ones, but the food isn't homemade. I contacted Ms. Raybourne, and she forwarded me a breakdown of food requirements for the team. I spent the day planning menus for us. We pick up the ingredients on our way home.

Besides, a thrift store is in the same shopping plaza as the grocery store. I want to check it out, and we should have enough time before Tabby's dance class to do both.

When I'm loading my purchases into the Range Rover, I notice how nice it is to have a larger trunk space. I also figure out how to connect my phone's Bluetooth to the speakers, and I let Tabby choose songs to listen to on the ride home. Back at Duke's house, a quick button press has the rear hatch lifting. It's easy to unload everything.

Maybe having access to the Range Rover will be nice for some things.

By the time I put the groceries and my thrift store purchases away the best I can, it's time to get Tabby ready for dance class. As we're leaving, I notice my car is back in the driveway with what appears to be new tires, so I move Tabby's booster seat over. We take it to dance, and I have to admit my car sounds much better after some attention. Still, I try not to notice how crappy it is compared to Duke's Range Rover.

On the ride, I ask Tabby about her day, but she's not very excited to talk about her time at school. I noticed the same thing last night when Duke asked her about her classes and teacher. She clams up. I allow her to drive the conversation. Something about a new game they played on the playground and a boy she beat in a foot race. But the closer we get to the dance studio, the quieter she becomes.

Duke sent me directions with a pointed request that I text when I arrive. Yesterday, I would have interpreted that as pushiness, but now I think he might just be a big worrywart.

The trip is uneventful, so I take a picture of Tabby walking up to the dance studio entrance, her bag hanging on her shoulder and her head down. I send the image to Duke. *We made it.*

We're early because I know nothing about how to put on her shoes and figured I would need the extra time. One of the other moms rescues me. She gives me the instructions on how to do it as I watch so I can help Tabby the next time. Tabby remains silent through the entire ordeal, only staring at the floor with a mixture of apprehension and dread. I don't understand what's going on, and I don't know what to ask her. At last, she joins the other girls as her instructor starts them through some sort of jazz warm-up.

Tabby skips along with her friends, and I assume her stiffness is because of her characteristic shyness. But by ten minutes in, she hasn't loosened up. At the twenty-minute mark, she's gone from stiff to agitated. At the end of the thirty-minute session, her face is a picture of relief.

She takes off her jazz shoes and puts her sneakers back on, plodding along next to me, back to the parking lot. Once she settles in the backseat in her booster, I head for her house. "So," I begin. "How long have you hated dance lessons?"

Her eyes become as big as quarters in my rearview mirror. "What? I didn't say I hated it."

I chuckle. "No, but I've seen people go to dentist appointments with more joy than you just tackled that dance lesson." She drops her head, staring at her hands. "How long have you been dancing?" I ask, trying again.

"I started in the spring." Her voice is small. If the radio was on, I might not have heard her.

My eyebrows lift as I glance back at her again in the mirror. "The spring? So, you've been taking lessons for about six months?" She nods. "If you don't hate it, then how do you feel about?"

She shrugs her small shoulders. "It's fine."

"Dancing? Dancing is only fine?" I can't keep the incredulity from my voice. Dancing is one of my favorite things. I've never been good at it, but that's never stopped me. "Dancing's the best."

"I like to dance." Tabby finally says. "But that kind of dancing is just boring." When I lift my brows in question, she continues. "There are so many rules." She sighs as if the weight of the world is on her shoulders. "Something that's supposed to be fun shouldn't have that many rules." She shakes her head. "It was my Nana's idea, though. My mom used to dance, I guess."

She must have run out of steam because she doesn't say anything else.

We drive along in silence. I read somewhere about Duke's wife. There's not much out there about her. Only that she died not long after Tabby was born. "There's no rule that we need to like the same things our parents like, you know." More than anyone, I know that. My mother's favorite things were gin, avoiding work, men who treated her like crap, and heavy eye makeup. We certainly aren't the same. "Have you told your father that you're not really enjoying it?"

"No."

"Why not?"

Again, the small shrug. "I don't want to bother him."

In the rearview, she isn't looking at me. She's staring out the window. I can only see her in profile, but I recognize the stubborn set to her jaw. I've seen it on her father's face a few times already.

"I think your dad will want to know this," I tell her softly, trying to figure out how I'll be able to help her with this. I don't understand the dynamic between father and daughter, and after our conversation last night, I'm not sure how to bring this up to Duke. But there's no reason that a young girl should have to take lessons she doesn't enjoy. After six months, she knows for sure how she feels about it. Most of all, communication is the foundation for every relationship—parental or otherwise. "What activities do you like to do, then?"

I don't expect a real answer, so I'm surprised when she offers one. "I kind of like team sports," she says to the window. "Like basketball and soccer. When we play them at school, I think that's fun. Most of the time, I play with the boys."

I try to remember what the front of her house looks like. "Do you guys have a basketball hoop somewhere that I didn't see?"

She shakes her head. "No. But there's one down the street at the playground."

I stop at a red light. "Well, how am I going to play with it down there?"

In the rearview mirror, she makes eye contact with me, and I cross my eyes at her. Her eyes crinkle, and I'm sure I catch a small grin. I'm coming to live for this little girl's smiles. "Lots of people get them in their driveway," I say. "Maybe we could too."

"Do you think so?" The smile she gives me might be her first genuine, wide-open one, and it makes happiness sing through me.

"I know so."

"Okay." She sounds uncertain, but she doesn't say more. We pull into the driveway, and I have a moment of victory. My clunker made it. *Take that, Duke.* I shift into park and turn off the car. "But don't tell Daddy."

"About the hoop?"

"No. That I don't like dance."

I turn in my seat and cock my head. "Why not?"

"He's busy."

"I'm sure your father wants to know what's going on."

She waves me off. "Yeah. But I need to watch out for him." She struggles with the door handle for a moment before she gets out, blissfully unaware that she left me speechless.

What kid thinks about their parent like that? Then again, by her age, I was practically raising myself. I never knew my father, and my mother and I moved from one short-term rental or hotel to another. I was too busy thinking about survival to worry about anything else. When my mom stopped coming home for the night when I was ten,

I even went to school for a few days with no one realizing I had no supervision. Until I got too hungry...

I shake my head. Duke asked me to give her space, worrying she wasn't tough enough to handle this change, and now she's protecting him in her seven-year-old way. It's obvious the two of them care about each other, but they both need to be honest with each other. Tiptoeing around what's important won't help them.

I watch as she heads through the side door, punching in the code. Chewing on my lower lip, I consider my options. Duke told me to charge whatever I needed. I pull up a shopping app and find the nicest basketball hoop I can, one I can change the height of the basket easily. I scan in his card and hit 'Buy Now.'

Quickly, I drop Duke a text. *Bought Tabby a basketball hoop. Receipt in your email. You said anything she needed.*

Hurrying out of the car, I catch up with Tabby at the door. "Hey," I call after her. "Do you want to help me make dinner?"

Her brow creases, but there's interest there, too. "I guess?"

"Perfect. Do you like chicken?"

Duke

IT'S RIGHT BEFORE TABBY'S bedtime when I get home from camp. A really long day. There's a note on the counter. *Dinner in the refrigerator.* June's script is swirly, slanting in a bunch of directions. She put a smiley face at the end. She still gave me a smile, even though I've been almost surly toward her. I grin in grudging admiration. I wonder if there's anything that phases this woman.

As I put the note back down and open the refrigerator, I admit how much I admire her spirit. Nothing seems to get her down. Or at least nothing seems to keep her that way. Hell, if she could put up with me the last few days, she can do about anything.

I lift the foil on top of the plate. It smells delicious. A peek at it shows chicken, sweet potatoes, and green beans. My mouth waters. I remove the foil, cover it with a paper towel, and put it in the microwave. As my dinner warms, I go in search of my chef nanny and my daughter. I find Tabby curled in the love seat in the playroom, a book in her hand.

"What are you doing?" I ask her, sliding into the love seat next to her. My quads are killing me. Keeping up with the young guys gets harder every year.

"Reading." She holds up her book, and there's a cartoon on the front. "June bought it for me."

"Did she?" I study the illustration on the front. "Is that a unicorn?"

"Da-ad," she drags the word out. "It's a narwhal." She snags her book back and points at the front. "And a jellyfish. Clearly." Opening the book, she finds her page and gets comfortable again.

"Clearly." Until now, we've read books together, and they're usually classics. *Frog and Toad*, the Narnia books, *Winnie the Pooh*. This is the first time she's tucked in like this with a book of her choosing. "Do you like it?"

She looks surprised. "I do." She smiles at the book and then at me. "It's funny, and there are lots of pictures." Shrugging, she goes back to her reading. Since she wants to get back to her book, I leave her to it. I go in search of June. I need to talk to her, anyway.

The door to her bedroom is open, so I pause outside of it and tap my knuckles against the door. "Knock knock." Immediately, I feel stupid. When did I lose my game?

She glances up from the laundry she's folding. "Hey. Did you need something?"

I'm not surprised she asks. I haven't exactly sought her out. But it still makes me feel shitty. "I wanted to thank you for getting the book for Tabby." I jut a thumb over my shoulder toward the playroom. "She's in there reading all alone. With no one telling her to do it."

"Do you usually have to force her to read?"

"Well, yeah. I keep offering her all sorts of stuff, but I don't really know what she would like. So, we just read what I liked as a kid."

"That's a good start." She cocks her head. "She probably loves reading with you. But if you want her to pick stuff up on her own, it's easier to give her a bunch of choices." She nudges her head toward the wall. There are stacks of dozens of books. "I picked all those up today so I could get a feel for where she is, what she likes."

I step inside so I can get a better look. "You bought all those for Tabby?" My credit card transactions pop up as notifications on my phone. I got something from an online sporting goods store after she texted me about a basketball hoop. There was something else from the grocery. Nothing about books. "I don't think I got the receipt for that."

She waves me off. "I went to the thrift store. You can get used books at places like that for ten cents or a quarter a piece. It takes some digging sometimes, but it's worth it." Her cheeks flush. "I read so much that it pays off to search. I exhausted the library stash, so if I want new titles, I will try there. Nerds got to get creative."

This version of her is irresistible. "I like to read too," I offer. "Nothing nerdy about that." Growing up, I used to get crap for how much time I spent with my nose in a book, but like everything else, I just didn't give a shit. I like the things I like, and fuck anyone who doesn't respect that.

"What do you like to read?" She asks.

I shrug. "Mostly sci-fi and fantasy. Some horror. Some nonfiction. It depends on my mood. You?"

"I like sci-fi and fantasy, too." She nods. "We didn't have many television channels when I was young. My teachers would let me borrow books from the school as long as I brought them back safely. I would read whatever was available, but I prefer paranormal or fantasy, especially if there's romance in it."

"You don't need to spend your money on my daughter's books." I step closer, and it's strange, being in her personal space. "It's kind of you, but I'm not paying you enough to buy her things."

Any excitement from talking about books a moment ago fades from her face. "I didn't mind. I was already there, looking for things for myself."

"Books?"

"Clothes." She folds her arms over her chest. "I buy secondhand if I can."

"You don't have to spend your money on Tabby. She's my daughter—"

"It was a gift, Duke." Her voice is teasing. "You know what gifts are, right? When you give someone something expecting nothing back? Tabby might be my charge, but I like her, and I wanted to do this for her. It's as simple as that." When I scowl at her, she laughs, rolling her eyes. "Besides, I just told you they were cheap. I probably spent five dollars or something on all of those books."

I direct my grimace to the stacks of books. They're uneven, leaning on one side. "You're sure?" It's a lot of books for five dollars.

"I'm sure. And whatever she doesn't like, I'll give to Lily. She likes to keep a library for the kids." She pauses, then adds, "if she ever has more kids again."

"Who's Lily?" I'm not generally a chatty guy, but it's hard to leave her room. I keep thinking of things I want to know.

"My foster mom until I aged out of the system. She lives in Moorestown." She goes back to folding the laundry on her bed. "Lived."

"How long did you live with her?" I notice what she's straightening. "Is that Tabby's shirt from yesterday?"

She waves me off. "I threw it in with my stuff when I was gathering this morning. I didn't have enough for a full load."

"We have a housekeeper. She does the laundry."

"Mrs. Reyes. I met her this morning. She's lovely." She smiles again, her big sunny grin.

"Yes, Mrs. Reyes." Now I cross my arms over my chest. "She cleans, does the laundry, stuff like that."

"She doesn't need to clean my clothes." She wrinkles her nose at me. "She only comes twice a week. What if I need something?" Shaking her head, she continues sorting. "I'll just do my own. It's not a big deal."

I continue watching her. After long minutes, she pauses, looking at me again. "What?"

"Nothing." I rub the back of my neck. "June. Um…" Why is this so hard to say? "I want to apologize. To you."

Her eyebrows lift so high I think they might disappear into her hair. She says nothing, though, only puts down the shirt she's folding and sits on her bed, watching me.

I guess I'm not getting any help from her. Not that I deserve it, but June's never struck me as the sort to sit quietly. I go on. "I screwed up. Today, when I took your car without asking and, well, since I've met you, actually."

"Huh," she offers.

That's not a real response. Her expression remains blank. I continue. "I would like what you offered last night."

"What did I offer last night?" I swear the side of her mouth twitches.

"You wanted to be friends," I grit out. "Would you still like to be friends?"

"With you?" She taps her pursed lips with her finger. "Let me think about it." She pauses. "Are you going to steal my car again?"

"No one wants to steal your car, Freckles."

She hums as if considering. "Do I still get to be cheerful? Oh, and I talk a lot. That's a nonnegotiable." She widens her eyes in mock innocence. "Talking's my favorite."

I throw up my hands. "I'm going to get Tabby through her shower."

She dissolves into laughter, and the sound of it makes my chest feel light. Today was so long, but now, with her giggling in front of me, it doesn't feel that bad.

"I'm sorry," she says. "You were just so serious."

I shake my head at her, but I can't help grinning back. I wave her off and head to the door.

Still chuckling, she calls after me. "Hey, Duke." I stop. "Thank you for saying that. Seriously."

Nodding, I roll my eyes, but I can't help smiling. Her shining eyes, her expressions... it's all too hard to resist. She closes her mouth to smother her laughter, as if she's trying to hold in her happiness, but it's there, in the crinkles around her eyes. Damned if watching this woman's happiness isn't the best feeling in the world.

But when she bites her lip, my gaze follows the movement, and heat slices through me. I clear my throat and glance away.

"Did you want me to get Tabby ready for bed?" she offers. Because of course she does. I shake my head.

"I'd like to catch up with her." As I move through the season, I won't get to spend as much time with Tabby. One drawback of this life.

"All right, then. Let me know if you need me."

I nod, and she returns to her laundry. The picture she paints—all homey and happy—is too cozy and appealing to me.

I run away.

June

THE NEXT MORNING WITH Tabby goes more smoothly than the first. She's still not a morning person, but she doesn't grumble as much. After I get her on the bus, I get dressed and go visit Lily at the assisted living facility. The drive from Haddonfield to Moorestown isn't long, especially when it isn't rush hour. I wave to the security guard at the gate and park behind the building. In the lobby, I hit the button for her apartment, and she buzzes me up. The door to her place is open when I arrive. "Mama. Are you here?"

Of course she is. She's not driving right now because of a recent toe amputation on her right foot. After the surgery, she spent a few weeks in a rehabilitation facility before they moved her to this place.

She wants to go home. When she had her stroke, she fell and broke her hip. After the surgery to repair it, the doctors struggled to stabilize her diabetes. The resultant setbacks ended in the toe amputation. It became clear she couldn't move back into her big, sprawling Victorian, so she agreed to sublet it to a military family for the school year to offset the costs. I moved her things into storage and set her up here.

It's a nice enough place. It's just not Lily's place.

"In here, June," she calls, and I follow the sound of her voice into the bedroom. Using her cane, she gets to her feet and throws her arms around me. She motions to the kitchen and her table. "Come. Sit. It's good to see you. It's too quiet in this darn place."

Until Lily's health deteriorated, and she ended up in the hospital, she still had three kids living with her. It broke her heart when the children had to be re-homed.

"You could turn on some music or something." I notice the radio is off, unusual for Lily. Usually, her space is full of delicious smells and music.

She waves me off. "I didn't feel like it." Lowering herself slowly to a chair, she sets her cane next to her, giving it a glare. "Stupid thing," she grumbles to it.

Lily's one of the most positive people I've ever met, so it's strange to see her irritable. I motion to the mug nearby. "Can I freshen up your coffee?"

"Please." She nods toward the kitchen. "I just brewed some."

I gather her cup and head to the counter. But the pot is off, and when I lift the carafe, it's cold. Rather than bring the discrepancy up to Lily, I discreetly dump the contents in the sink next to me and refill the water. In record time, I've got a new pot brewing, and I join Lily at the table.

Covering her older hands with mine, I meet her brown eyes. "All right. Out with it. What's going on?"

She grimaces. "I'm that obvious, huh?"

"It's not a bad thing to have an open face." I grin at her. "You've always told me that."

"It's the truth too. But it's sure inconvenient sometimes," she grumbles.

"Tell me about it," I say, rolling my eyes. She smiles, my desired effect.

"I need to start dialysis."

"What?" I sit up straighter in my chair. "When? When did you find out? What happened?" I pause, considering. She had a doctor's appointment earlier in the week. "Why didn't you tell me sooner?"

She lifts her hand. "Now, Junie. Stop worrying."

"Dialysis. That's for your kidneys, correct?" I run through the information her doctor gave us the last time we were in about how her diabetes needs to be controlled or she's bound for more complications. "But that's for kidney failure. Are your kidneys failing?" My mind races, panic taking hold. I thought things with her were looking up. She's getting around better with her cane. She doesn't love it, but I thought we were on an upswing.

"That's what the doctor told me, yes."

"Oh, shit."

"June Harlow. Language."

"Right. Sorry." I run a hand over my hair, from forehead to the end of my ponytail, my mind racing. "What happens now?"

"I'll need to visit the office three times a week to have it done."

"Three times a week?" My head spins. That's so much.

"Yes. For a few hours each time."

"But how are you going to get there?"

"I've arranged for senior transport."

I shake my head. "No. I can drive you."

"You just started your new job, June." Lily covers my hand with hers. "You can't be spending four hours, three days a week, sitting with me at a dialysis center." She leans back. "Tell me more about your charge. Tabby. What's she like?"

"She's amazing, but already I can tell she's struggling in school." I point at her. "But you're changing the subject. I'm sure I can take you, at least sometimes. I have a lot of flexibility. Tabby's in school all day. I can take you over, sit with you, and be back in time for her to get off the bus."

"June—"

"At least a couple times a week," I insist. "I'll just talk to Duke. Please. Let me help." I hate the idea of her riding back and forth, sitting there for hours, all alone.

She flattens her lips. "I can do it by myself, you know." Her brow furrows, and I'm sure she doesn't mean the words to be hurtful, but they sting.

"I know you can," I whisper. "But I want to help."

Her eyes soften. "Of course, dear. I know you do." She smiles, and I try to return it, but my attempt feels sickly. "I'll adjust the schedule, but only after you check with your new boss."

"Okay. I'm sure Duke won't mind." At the mention of Duke, my face heats. Ugh, stupid complexion.

"Duke, huh?" Lily narrows her eyes, and I resist the urge to squirm. "Tell me more about him."

"Well, he's a hockey player." My cheeks are burning. "He's the captain," I offer, latching on to innocuous information.

"Is he now?" It's obvious Lily's not fooled. "And what does he look like?"

"Lily..."

She laughs, and it's so good to hear.

I grin back at her. "Fine. He's handsome." She lifts her brows. "Okay, he's the most good-looking man I've ever met." Nodding, she grins knowingly. "In my defense, he works out all the time, so of course he has an amazing body."

"Of course."

"And the rest of it... the good bone structure, his amazing hands, good skin... that's probably his diet, right?"

"Probably." She chuckles, propping her chin in her hands.

I roll my eyes. "Now you're patronizing me."

She laughs again. "You know, it's okay if you find him attractive."

"No, it's not okay. He's my boss." Last night, I steered clear of Duke and Tabby except to hug Tabby good night. After his apology, I needed a chance to regroup. I couldn't help teasing him. He's so serious all the time. But I didn't expect how his smile would affect me, how seeing him relax filled me with equal parts desire to curl up in a ball next to him and just desire desire.

When that man's face softens into a lazy grin, he screams sex like a sign at an adult bookstore.

But what really got me was the surprise on his face when he realized we were laughing together. I don't think Duke York relaxes with many people, and that tugged at my heart.

Lily cuts into my musings. "When I worked at the diner, when I was a girl, I thought my boss was attractive."

"You did?"

"Sure. It's not like they stop looking the way they do just because they're your boss."

"That doesn't help me, Lily."

"I'm not trying to help you, hon." She pats my hand. "And, in fact, I'm not even going to judge you. I can't even remember the last time you thought someone was attractive. I'm happy to hear it."

"That's not good parental advice. You're supposed to tell me it's unprofessional to be checking out my boss." I thought I was coming here to check my moral compass.

She waves me off. "June, I've never had to point you in the right direction. You've always been so eager to do the right thing. I've just stood by and let you work it out on your own."

"That's not true." I sit up straighter. "You know I always come to you for advice."

"You do. But it's mostly just to talk things over. You need a sounding board, not a guide. Half the time, I get as much out of our conversations as you do."

I consider that. Lily has never been an overbearing or pushy guardian. "Maybe you just remind me what the right path should be."

"Maybe, girl. Maybe." She pats my cheek. "So, what does your conscience tell you about this Duke?"

"I should stay away from him," I admit. "He's my boss, and he has a seven-year-old daughter. There's too much complicated about it."

She tilts her head. "That's true."

I sigh. "Yes. Yes, it is." Unable to sit still any longer, I get up and pour Lily her coffee. Setting the steaming mug in front of her, she covers my fingers as she takes it.

Staring up at me, her smile is sad. "But sometimes our heart doesn't listen to our head, does it?"

It's not my heart that's preoccupied with Duke York's hot body. But that's not a suitable response, so I hum noncommittally and change the subject. "When does your dialysis start?"

Lily allows the switched topic, and we discuss her treatments and what the doctors have said. When I leave, I promise to drive her to her first appointment tomorrow. She agrees.

"Oh," I say, as I am heading for the door. "Would you mind if I borrow some of the kids' books from storage? I'm trying to get a feeling for what Tabby enjoys reading."

Lily smiles. "No one else is reading them right now."

As I drive home, I consider what Lily said. Sure, the heart doesn't always listen. But the head decides, and common sense says all there can be between Duke and me is a friendly working relationship.

Harry Styles's "Music for a Sushi Restaurant" blares from the speakers in the kitchen. Next to me, Tabby stands on one of the dining room chairs, her hands covered in flour. For dinner tonight, I'm showing Tabby how to make homemade pasta. It also serves as a stealthy way to observe how she reads and works with numbers from the recipe. But we're having so much fun, I don't think she realizes I'm quizzing her.

I throw my head back and sing along. "Baaaa, ba ba…" The whole time, I wiggle my butt, stirring the meatballs, checking the pasta water, and dancing along at the same time. When I shimmy back to Tabby, she's all skepticism. "What?"

"You know you're not a good singer, right?" She says, her eyes narrowed.

I sputter a laugh. "I'm not?" Pressing a hand to my chest, I stare at her wide-eyed. "Seriously?" She shakes her head, and I crack up. I know I'm tone deaf. That's never stopped me from singing. I figure that if the powers that be gave me this voice, they deserve to hear it.

"You can't dance either, June," she tells me matter of fact, squishing her hands into the pasta dough. "You are way offbeat."

This is something else I am aware of. I love music, but dancing isn't one of my skills. Like with sports and other physical activities, I've never had natural grace. Still, I love the way the beats feel in my body, so I move anyway.

She hops down off the chair, and I say nothing when she wipes her hands on her shirt. She started this conversation, and she's talking to me willingly. I'm taking the win. "Let me show you a few things."

Shaking my head, I hold up my hands. "Oh, hon, trust me. People have tried to teach me. I'm a hopeless case."

"Daddy says you can do anything with enough practice." That sounds exactly like something a professional athlete might say, even though my guess is he was born with at least some—if not a lot—of natural talent. "All you need is the right teacher."

I resist the urge to grin at her. She sounds adorable parroting her father. "Maybe that's it then. So... show me what you've got, kid."

While the pasta dough rests, Tabby tries to explain a step-ball-change move to me. I do my best—truly I do—but though she's light on her feet and unfailingly patient, I just can't get it.

"Is this what you're learning at dance class, Tabby Cat?" Duke's voice surprises me, and I almost trip myself in the middle of another failed dance step attempt. I'm pleased when I stay upright. Duke leans against the door to the kitchen. He looks comfy, and I don't know how long he's witnessed my flailing. "You are an excellent teacher."

His daughter sighs. "I'm not sure, Daddy. She's still really terrible."

I laugh, but then Duke's eyes find mine. Once again, that unfamiliar flutter reaches through my stomach. He's my boss, though, and I'm certain that stomach tingles are an unprofessional reaction to my employer.

Focus on friendship.

Nervously, I swipe the stray hair around my face behind my ears and laugh. "My terribleness has nothing to do with the teacher and everything to do with the student."

He motions toward the speakers. "What are we listening to?"

"Harry Styles, Dad." Tabby's voice implies a duh at the end. The sushi restaurant song has ended, and now Styles is singing about watermelons. "June let me pick."

"Did she?" He lifts his eyebrows at me.

I shrug. "I like Harry too."

"Harry, is it?"

"We could be on a first-name basis. You don't know. Harry and I could be friends."

He barks out a laugh, and the effect on his face steals my breath. If Duke is appealing when he's broody, he's irresistible when he smiles.

"Maybe you should help her, Dad." Tabby steps to the side and waves her father toward me. "You're a good dancer. Maybe she just needs another teacher."

My gaze darts to Duke. "Oh no. I don't think so." I sound panicked because I am. When Duke came into the kitchen, his face was neutral, almost like everything was normal. Like we're friends. But nothing could derail that faster than having him put his hands on me.

If looking at him makes my stomach tingle, I don't want to know how I'll feel if he touches me.

"Daddy's really good, June." Tabby's looking up at me with wide eyes, oblivious. "Sometimes we just need a different teacher."

I bet there are a lot of things Duke York could show me. I blow out a breath. Since leaving Lily's earlier, I've had more than a couple of inappropriate thoughts about him. I need to keep my head in the game.

I smile at Tabby and retreat to the stove. The meatballs are an excuse to step away from Duke. "I'm going to practice what you showed me first, Tabby." When I get the nerve to make eye contact with him again, I can't read the look on his face. "We're making pasta," I say to change the subject. "Tabby said you both like pasta. I made it with whole wheat flour. Complex carbs."

I press my lips together, forcing myself to stop talking. Of course, they like pasta. Most people like pasta.

"You're making dinner again." It's not a question, more like an observation.

"Yes." I glance around the kitchen. There's dough on the island and meatballs simmering on the stove. "Pasta."

"Pasta, not from a box."

"Pasta doesn't start in a box, you know," I inform him. "Someone puts it there."

"Not someone, I bet." Tabby hikes herself up on a kitchen stool. "A machine, probably."

I nod. "You're right. Probably a machine."

"You're going to make homemade pasta, though?" He drops a workout bag at the door and straddles a second stool. He studies the contents on the island in front of us with interest.

"Technically, Tabby made the dough." I grin at her, and she nods, her head tilting up in pride. "And I'm going to use your pasta attachment to make the noodles."

"My pasta attachment?" He sits up straighter. "What pasta attachment?"

The piece of equipment is behind me, and I snag it. "I found it in a drawer when I was searching for utensils. I hope that's okay. Tabby has been showing me around, but I've been sort of just digging—"

"June." He stops me and then softens his face into a smile. "It's fine. You live here."

Ugh, his smile is ridiculous. "It's a pasta press."

"It is?" He looks genuinely confused. "Huh."

"It's in your kitchen. You don't know what it is?" I look around. "Is there anyone else who cooks here?"

"Nana cooks sometimes," Tabby pipes up. "But she's not very good at it." Her face brightens up. "Like you're not a good dancer!"

"Tabby..." Her father's voice holds censure, but I crack up.

"She's not wrong," I say. "We are all special in our own way." Duke presses his fingers to his eyes, like this conversation is giving him a headache, but he can't hide his grin. "Does Nana live nearby?" I read he was from Canada, but his wife was from Philadelphia. Duke mentioned his mother-in-law was recovering from a broken leg.

"Yep. She lives in Haddonfield too."

"That must be nice."

"Do you know how that works?" Duke interrupts us, studying the attachment in my hand with a furrowed brow. I recognize the skepticism. I've already seen it on his daughter's face. It's doubtful they realize how similar their mannerisms are, but every time I see a similarity, it makes me happy because it means I'm getting to know them.

"I think I've got it," I say. Lily is Italian, and we made lots of pasta by scratch. Her tools are older, not as high tech, but I feel confident. "Why don't you help me put the dough in, Tabby?"

I can tell it surprises Duke how fast his daughter gets up to join me. We get caught up in the bustle of making the noodles, and Duke hangs out with us. He doesn't say much, but I'm sure he smiles at Tabby at least once. I suggest we eat in the dining room, and Tabby treats it like an adventure. We make up our plates and head to the table. Like every other room in the house, this one is tasteful, but it's not untouchable.

"How was everyone's day?" I ask. Lily used to insist we eat dinner together, and she made sure we always modeled pleasant dinner conversation. The entire time I lived with her, from age ten until I went to college, other foster kids constantly cycled through the house. Dinnertime was a constant. No tech, no music, no television or distractions of any kind. We would sit together and talk. If we were in after-school activities and couldn't make dinnertime, she would save us leftovers and sit with us, if she could. She said it was a time to reconnect.

Duke looks surprised. "Good?"

"That's not really an answer," I tell him. "Tell me more. It's the first week of camp. How is that going?"

He finishes chewing and glances at me and Tabby. "Well, it's kind of..." He seems to catch himself. "It's a mess, actually."

"Why?" I always figured training camps for professional athletes were more of a formality than anything else. The athletes get paid to play games. It seems like training must be an afterthought.

"The veterans. A lot of the old guys came back not looking like they did anything this off-season." He stabs a forkful of pasta and shoves it in his mouth.

"Why the veterans?" I would assume experienced players would take their job more seriously.

"Last year was a rough one, and I think a lot of them tried to pretend it didn't happen. Now that reality is hitting, they're regretting their life choices."

"Oh." I take another bite and consider. "Why was last year rough?"

He tilts his head. "You really don't know much about hockey, do you?"

I shrug. "No. I really don't." I motion with my fork. "I work a lot. And when I don't work, I was in school. It has left little time for following sports or television shows or whatever."

"What do you do for fun?"

"I read, like I told you." I shovel another bite of food into my mouth. The pasta turned out well, if I say so myself.

He makes a noncommittal grunt, and then he answers. "Last year was hard because we had a couple of guys on the team who were more interested in making headlines and getting endorsement deals than they were in winning games." His lips thin. "I didn't appreciate them turning our team into a circus."

I nod and decide to look that up later. As Duke continues to eat, I get the basic idea. He's a serious guy, and I bet he takes his job seriously, too. He's the captain. That means he holds a leadership role. I bet having members of his team who lacked the same commitment bothered him.

"And this year?"

"Management traded most of the biggest offenders." When I tilt my head in question, he explains. "The coaches didn't like the drama either. This isn't a town or organization that puts up with a lot of nonsense. Our fans want us to come in and work hard for them. The rest of it was a distraction." He moves his pasta around to get the last forkfuls. "But they decided not to invest in any other big name players. Instead, they drafted some prospects, signed some young guys who had been top draft picks out of college, and called some players up from the minors. It's obvious they want to rebuild. It's just making for a weird mix of the old guard and a bunch of young rookies."

"There must be a big discrepancy in experience, then." I'm trying hard to understand the dynamic.

"Yeah." He snorts. "Like, a bunch of overeager newbies and some leftover cynical d—dummies." He catches himself before the last word and glances at Tabby, as if reminding himself she's there. She's busy scarfing down her dinner.

"Right. Dummies." I meet his eyes and grin. We both know he wasn't going to say that.

Tabby drops her fork. "I'm done, Dad. Can I go watch a show?"

"Do you have homework?"

"I'm in second grade." She rolls her eyes and gets up. "No."

"Take your plate to the sink, then." She nods, collects her dish, and scurries toward the family room. She drops her plate in the sink, as requested.

In the silence, I search for new conversation starters. I rarely struggle with this. But with Tabby gone, I'm intensely aware of him, and it's shorting out my brain.

Even my rare dates aren't this full of tension. He's not the only super hot and talented person I've ever met. He might be the most blatantly sexy, but Duke's my boss, my charge's father. Why doesn't my stupid body know he's totally off-limits? If my body doesn't get it, my brain certainly should and be able to come up with some bit of thoughtful conversation.

Nothing.

We sit there in awkward silence for long minutes until he finally says, "Thank you."

"For what?" I ask.

"Dinner." He motions to his plate, which is completely empty. "I don't eat a lot of pasta."

"No?"

"No." He chuckles, and the sound warms my belly. Stupid belly. "Carbs," he offers as explanation.

I swallow hard. "Carbs. Right."

"But this was really delicious. Did you make those meatballs too?" His voice is soft, and it soothes me. I nod, my mouth so dry. "Those were perfect. I don't think I've ever had better."

I grin, waving him off. "Please, you can eat anywhere you want, I'm sure you've—"

He places his hand over mine, and when his brown eyes meet mine, the words die in my mouth. "I could, and I do eat lots of places. In the off-season, it's pretty basic here. Or we eat from the food service the team recommends. My mom wasn't a great cook, so she didn't teach me much. And as Tabby said, Sonya's mom is worse. I figured I'd teach myself how to do more than scramble eggs and heat soup, but so far I haven't. I appreciate this."

Lifting his hand from mine, he rubs the back of his neck like he's uneasy. Definitely not comfortable sharing his thoughts. It's really a small thing—to thank someone for dinner—but the rest of what he said feels private, and that touches me.

"You know," I say, clasping my hands together to distract from the tingling feeling that's still there from where we touched. "If you're having problems getting the guys to work together, maybe we could host a team bonding party or something."

"You want to host a party. For me."

I scowl at him. He makes these kinds of statements, but it's really a question. Like he's surprised I've said something, so he's just checking to make sure he heard me right.

"Yeah." I'm warming to the idea. "You guys have a pool, right? And this house is enormous. The yard's gigantic too." I took a few minutes to wander around outside this morning. "We could have a barbecue. It's still September and boiling hot. We could do it right before the season opener, if you wanted."

He shakes his head. "That's a lot of work, don't you think?"

I wave him off. "How many guys are on your roster?"

"We have twenty-three guys on our active roster."

I do some quick calculations. "Some of them are married?"

"Half maybe? Some kids, but not too many."

That doesn't sound so bad. I've got lots of experience feeding sizable crowds. "Let's do it. I can cook stuff and—" I'm already excited. I love throwing a party.

"June, I don't know."

"Come on, Duke. It'll help your team, right?"

He shrugs sheepishly. "Yeah. Maybe. Probably."

"And you said you want your teammates to mesh. That it's important, after last year."

"Well, yes."

"It would be fun." I put my hands on the table. "And it'll give Tabby and me something to do together."

His scowl is back. "I'll think about it." He stands, and when I try to convince him further, he lifts his hands. "Please. We'll talk about it tomorrow."

I get the impression he's had enough for the day, so I let it go. He leans back so he can see Tabby in the living room. I follow his gaze and catch sight of her on the couch, her bare feet swinging over the side. A cartoon is on television, but it's been a few years since I watched any. I'm not familiar with the popular ones right now.

Duke moves to stand. "Let me help with the dishes." There are dark smudges under his eyes.

I wave him off. "I got it. You had a long day. You can help me tomorrow."

He stretches, wincing. He's not yet thirty, but sometimes he moves like a much older person. "Are you sure?"

"Absolutely."

He mumbles something that sounds like "I need to watch film," but he stops again on his way upstairs. "Thank you, June. For dinner and the dishes. I appreciate it." In the dim light from the hall, he looks almost vulnerable. Usually, I would say something to diffuse the seriousness on his face, but I can't right now. He raps his knuckles on the doorway and heads toward his office.

I watch him go.

Duke York isn't what I expected.

Duke

In my office, I stretch out on the couch and prepare to dig into the film Coach Hargreeves sent me. Some teams in our division have gone through major overhauls like ours, so we have little information about them yet. But there are a handful of teams whose core players are the same this year. I figured I would get a jump on preparing for them now. But my mind wanders to the beautiful woman living in my house.

Watching Tabby with June in the kitchen tonight was eye-opening. Seeing them working side by side, singing, cemented what I think I always knew—June is exactly what Tabby needs. My daughter seems more at ease with her than I've ever seen her be with someone new. She's always been an excellent judge of character, and if Tabby is comfortable with her this quickly, June Harlow is the real thing.

It's me who's the problem. Because June makes me anything but comfortable around her. Damned if watching her dancing in the kitchen, singing so off-key it was nearly painful to hear, didn't fill me with an entire bag of unwelcome feelings. First, she's the fucking hottest thing I've ever seen, and I've met my fair share of beautiful women. But June's not manufactured beauty. Everything about her is unassuming, and I find the effect more appealing than if she wore the fanciest clothes and makeup. Tonight, she puttered around my kitchen in leggings and her Rutgers University T-shirt, with her hair in a messy bun, and I haven't been so attracted to anyone in years.

It's not how she looks, though. It's how she gets Tabby to smile, the way she dives right into things. I haven't exactly been welcoming to her, but she offered to help me throw a party. I've hosted nothing like that before, and I wouldn't know where to start. Sonya was always the entertainer, the one with the open smile. She hadn't been extroverted—far from it—but she was genuine. I'm not social like that. The closest I've gotten to hosting is inviting a few of the guys over to watch whatever sports are on television. That usually comprises ordering a pizza and getting some beer.

When she brought up a barbecue, my entire body flinched. I can't even imagine the caterers involved, the decorations... I shiver. It sounds like a nightmare, yet she said it would be fun. I can't tell if she's serious.

But that's what tonight in the kitchen was. Watching the two of them dance and banter... it was fun. And June did that for my daughter. For the first time, I think maybe, just maybe, this might work out.

That leaves me hopeful, and I start a video. Camp must be getting to me more than I thought, though, because I doze off. I vaguely recall Tabby crawling in my lap to kiss me good night, and I'm sure I must be dreaming when June's soft whisper calls to her.

I'm groggy and disoriented when I wake later. It's pitch-black outside the windows, and the only light on is next to the desk. I didn't turn it on, so June must have done it. She let me sleep.

My watch says it's after midnight. I rub my eyes and stretch. Damn, only six more hours until I need to get to the rink to run my guys.

I plug in my tablet and turn off the lights downstairs. Closing the French doors to the room, I head up to bed, doing my best to ignore the creaks and aches in my body. I hate the constant reminders of how old I'm getting. I stop outside Tabby's door. She's spread out like a starfish in the center of the bed, her blond hair a messy halo around her head. She looks so much like her mother most days, but especially when she's sleeping and her face is soft.

As quietly as I can manage, I creep in and do my best to cover her, but it's hard with the blankets tangled around her. When I'm satisfied she won't freeze overnight, I tiptoe back out to the hall, leaving the door open like she prefers.

As I head down the hall toward my room, I notice a light on in the upstairs playroom, filtering through the crack left by the half-open door. I glance in.

On the overstuffed love seat in the corner, June's curled up in a ball, sound asleep.

I pause. Maybe I shouldn't go in. She obviously came in here to be alone, so I should probably leave her to it. After all, no one uses this room much anymore. Until I saw Tabby in here reading in the same spot the other day, I don't know if anyone had been in here in months. When Tabby was small, we kept a bunch of toys up here as well as in the play area downstairs, so she could be on whichever floor I was on. But the older she gets, the less she's come here, preferring to keep her favorite toys closer, in her room or in the living room.

But June could be chilly. We set the air conditioning on high. Both Tabby and I like to sleep cold. It won't hurt anything if I go in and check on her.

I'm standing in my fucking upstairs hallway, second-guessing myself. Since when am I this guy? I'm known for being decisive, a leader on my team. I'm raising a daughter on my own. Logically, it makes sense to check on June. She's new in the house, and it's my job to make sure she's safe and comfortable.

Decided, I push through the door. The only light on is over her chair, and I notice her phone lying next to her face. She must have been reading something or watching something and dozed off, too.

In sleep, she looks angelic. When she's awake, she's full of energy. Now, with her features soft, she could be right out of a painting. Her hair twists over her shoulder, and her freckles cover most of her face. The urge to touch her is almost unbearable, but I keep my hands to my fucking self.

Huck was right yesterday. June is a distraction. I need to be focused and on top of my game. Not only is this my last chance, but my team deserves my best. And June doesn't deserve to have her employer bothering her.

It would be easiest if I could just not find her attractive, but that won't be an option. I want her. I have since I saw her in Raybourne's office. No amount of pretending is going to change that fact, and I doubt there's going to be any way for me to stop it. This woman is like a rainbow after a storm, an unrelenting spark of light in our life. Until she got here, I didn't think we needed anything like that. Tabby and I... we do okay. We're happy, I think. But June? She's glitter, making everything sparkle.

All that is true, but if there's one thing I am, it's disciplined. I can stay away from her, compartmentalize. The good she will do for Tabby is worth the effort to stay away from her. Nothing has the potential to send June away more than if I mix business with pleasure. I haven't seen my daughter as happy as she was tonight in a long time, and I won't do anything to jeopardize that.

Glancing around the room, I spot the ottoman where we store blankets. I open it and grab the thickest, fluffiest one. Gently, I tuck it around my sleeping nanny, and I force myself to step away.

Turning off the light, I leave, pulling the door closed behind me.

June

Duke is gone by the time I get Tabby up on Thursday morning. I'm glad because it gives me a moment to get my bearings.

There's a cozy love seat in the playroom upstairs, so I sat down to read last night. I'm in the middle of the second book in a young adult fantasy series, and I want to finish it before the final book comes out next week. I guess I didn't make it, because I woke up after two in the morning, my phone on the floor. But that wasn't unusual. I've fallen asleep reading more times than I can count. What was strange is that I woke up toasty warm with a blanket draped over me.

I didn't put it there, and I can't imagine Tabby did either. Which leaves Duke.

It's not a huge deal. Lots of people would see someone sleeping and think about covering them. But Duke did it. That fills me with the fuzzy feeling in my belly again, and I shouldn't be thinking warm and fuzzy thoughts about my boss.

That afternoon, I pick Tabby up at school. Duke has already introduced me to her teacher via email, as well as giving her permission to discuss Tabby with me, but I want to put a face with the name. If Tabby is having problems, I want Miss Shepherd to know we're involved and open to her suggestions.

After I gather Tabby at the walkers' exit, I ask her to show me to her room. She's not excited at first, but when I point out how cool it'll be to see her school with no one in it, her curiosity gets the better of her. We sign in at the office, and she walks me through the winding halls to her classroom. Luckily, the lights are still on. I knock on the open door. "Hello? Miss Shepherd?"

A curly-haired woman pops her head out from where she's kneeling behind a closet door. "Hello?"

Beside me, Tabby has clammed up. Her chin is on her chest, and her hair, which has escaped the braid I put it in this morning, is around her face. I wave, stepping inside. "Hi, Miss Shepherd. I'm June Harlow, Tabby's nanny. I emailed you earlier this week, but I wanted to come in and meet you in person."

Miss Shepherd stands, a warm smile on her face, and dusts her hands on her pants. "Of course." She extends a hand, and we shake. "Nice to meet you." She squats in front of Tabby. "Hey, Tabby. Good job today on your art project. I love what you did." She points to the row of smiling cats painted in primary colors hanging on the wall. Tabby shrugs. Miss Shepherd glances at me, and then she points to the corner, where there are books and pillows strewn in a reading nook. "Would you do me a favor, Tabby? Could you please tidy the Reading Corner? I could really use the help."

She nods, shuffling over to the brightly colored pillows and tables, and starts organizing. Miss Shepherd motions toward her desk, and I follow her. "I'm so glad you could come in to see me."

"Of course. I just graduated from Rutgers with dual elementary education and special education degrees. I know how important it is to have good home-to-school communication." Miss Shepherd hums in agreement. I motion around the room. "I would be happy to come in and help in any way you need. Mystery reader, helping with parties, field trips, whatever. Please don't hesitate to reach out."

"Thank you. That means so much."

"I wanted to see how Tabby is doing so far. Her father and I want to make sure you know we're here to support her."

"I'm glad you did. I planned to reach out in the next week, anyway." She opens a drawer and rifles through a filing cabinet of folders, selecting one. It has Tabby's name written on the tab. "Last year, Tabby's teacher suggested they place Tabby in our inclusion room. She's not a classified student, but the teacher thought it might be good to have her in a room where there would be two teachers, so we could have double eyes on her if she continued to struggle."

I know that inclusion rooms are the same as single-teacher rooms in a school, but they have a second certified special education teacher present who makes sure students with special needs have them met—through extra time, modifications, emotional support, or any other help.

Miss Shepherd opens the file and pulls out a few pieces of paper. They're tests and classwork, and none of the grades are good. They aren't all failing, but they're consistently low. Since the work isn't very difficult, I suspect Tabby could guess at every answer and get about half of them right.

"These are her most recent math grades." She slides two pieces of paper toward me. There are some corrections, but she manages Bs and Cs. "And this is her most recent word work." She opens a composition book. The writing on the pages is rudimentary, even considering the age and academic level. Educators expect a certain amount of misspellings at her age, but Tabby's writing lacks spacing between the words. Most of it is a string of letters. She capitalized some letters and placed a period before each of them. But the capitalization doesn't make much sense, and the periods are out of place.

"I see." I do, actually. Tabby's writing suggests some sort of learning disability. I'm not able to diagnose it, but I've studied enough to know if something is wrong.

Miss Shepherd holds my gaze before tucking the work back into Tabby's folder and closing it. "She's struggling, Miss Harlow. My resource teacher and I don't know exactly how, but Tabby closes down more every day. She struggles to concentrate, and when she gives her work attention, it's difficult for her." She inhales. "We would like to refer her to the child study team."

"I see." I glance across the room at Tabby, and my chest aches. Last year's progress reports suggested a problem, but to hear it confirmed, to see the full extent, it breaks my heart. She's a quiet kid, but I can already tell she's very sensitive and intuitive. Undoubtedly, she can tell something is wrong. At seven, feeling different can be very difficult.

"I'm going to send home the Vanderbilt diagnostic scale. Are you familiar with it?" I nod. Doctors and educators use the assessment to determine if someone is at risk of ADHD. It asks questions about the student's behaviors both in and out of the classroom. It's usually the first step toward school intervention. "Good. I'll send two copies, one for you and one for Mr. York. Please return them as soon as possible."

"I will." I smile and nod before sticking out my hand to her. "And keep in mind what I said about helping. I want to be present here."

"Thank you. We would love that," she says and shakes my hand.

I join Tabby and help her finish her task. As we leave, walking side by side down the hallway, she sighs.

"You wanted to meet Miss Shepherd because of me, didn't you?" she asks.

I squeeze her shoulder. "Of course. I wanted to know your teacher."

"No." Her shoulders hunch over a little. "I mean because I'm stupid."

My heart pounding, I stop, reaching for her hand and halting her with me. Squatting down, I look in her eyes, still holding her hand. "You're not stupid at all," I say, steel in my voice. "Why would you say that?"

She shrugs. "That's what the kids at school think. They don't say it, but I can tell." Her mouth twists, like she's trying to keep it from shaking. "I'm not like the rest of them."

My eyes sting, but I hold it together. She doesn't need my emotions right now. Her own are probably overwhelming enough. I want to step in, to tell her she fits in, that she is like the rest of them. But it doesn't matter if I believe that. It's her perspective that matters. "Why not?"

"I don't think like they do."

The words are devastating, and she heads off down the hall, walking too fast. She doesn't stop until she pushes through the exit, coming to a halt on the pavement outside the door. She tilts her head up to the sky and inhales a deep breath, like there hadn't been enough oxygen in the school.

Biting my lower lip to keep from crying, I glance back at the classroom.

Whatever is going on with Tabby, I'm going to help her work through it. There is nothing in me that will allow that smart, sweet girl to feel like this for much longer.

Duke

It's dusk when I get home from training camp. I got dragged into three different meetings, and I'm completely exhausted by the time I pull into the driveway. But the sight of June covered in sweat wakes me up. She's got on short shorts and a T-shirt, and her hair is in a messy ponytail. We've been going through an uncharacteristic heat wave, so it's still over eighty degrees. She wipes her brow with her forearm and stands. Around her are the remnants of a cardboard box and what appears to be the start of a basketball hoop.

I kill the engine, throw open the door, and step out. "What's going on?"

She dusts off her palms. "I'm putting together a basketball hoop." She motions to the side yard where Tabby plays on the swing set. "Tab told me she would help, but she abandoned me."

"I see that." I put my hands on my hips. "How's it going?"

"Well, I was good until the lettering on the pieces didn't align with the picture of the pieces. And I found a wrench, but it's not the right size. So, I was about to go back into the garage to find another one." She glares at the tool in her hand, as if the wrench purposely changed sizes to be difficult.

"Why didn't you wait for me?"

She glares at me. "Because it didn't say this was a two-person job. I put lots of stuff together for Lily. There was no reason to believe I couldn't handle it."

"You don't always need to handle everything on your own, you know."

She snorts and squats back down next to the net.

Her non-agreement bothers me, so I stoop down next to her. Her skin flushes from the heat and being this close fills me with the need to touch her. "I'm serious."

"You like to ask for help?" She tilts her head, lifting an eyebrow at me. Her hazel eyes narrow. "Because you weren't exactly excited to have me here to help you, even though you are the one who hired me."

"I already apologized for that." I pick up the instructions.

"Yes, you did. I'm pointing out that maybe both of us could use some help asking for help." She puts the wrench down and pushes her hair out of her face.

"Fair." I hand her the instructions. They make no sense to me. "Well, I might suck at asking for help, but I can get you the right wrench."

She grins at me, taking the instructions from my hand. "I'd appreciate that."

I stand up, heading toward the garage. I'm not really sure what kind of wrench she needs, but I figure I can grab a few different sizes and let her choose. As I walk, my mind drifts back to our conversation. She's right. I don't always ask for help when I need it. I've always prided myself on being independent, but maybe that's not always a good thing. Maybe it's time to lean on others a little more.

I find a set of wrenches and head back to the driveway. June stretches, rubbing her neck, her eyes on Tabby. My daughter is swinging, and she appears to be singing to herself. I chuckle.

"Harry Styles?" I ask, coming up behind June. Her brow creases in question. I point to Tabby. "She's singing. I was wondering if the song is by your friend Harry."

She offers me another of her sexy grins. "On the way home from school, she belted out every word of Taylor Swift's new song. She's pretty good."

I chuckle, taking in the sight. Something about seeing June and Tabby together warms my heart. Maybe it's the fact they bring out a different side of me, a side I never knew existed. I hand June the wrenches and watch as she expertly picks out the right size.

"Thanks." She motions to the net. "Would you like to help me? Put it together, I mean? I could use the help."

"I thought you'd never ask."

She grins at me, and I can't help smiling back.

We work together, June reading the instructions and doing the complex work, while I mostly add the muscle. It's not long before the hoop is complete, and we hang the net.

"I think we did a good job," she says, wiping the sweat from her forehead. "Now I need to order a basketball."

"You haven't already?" I've been watching the charges go by on my credit card and checking the receipts she's sent me. There are a few school workbooks, some toys, lots of groceries, and this hoop. This morning, she sent me a bill for a soccer ball. I can't believe we didn't already have one, but if she bought it, I assume we didn't.

"I needed to figure out what size to get her. I never played basketball, so I need to look it up."

"I can do it," I offer. "I played when I was younger."

"You played basketball and hockey?"

I shrug. "I played basketball until I got serious about hockey in middle school. Same with soccer, baseball. I even ran track for a while."

She shakes her head, laughing. "I didn't play any of those things."

"Why?" Most kids try at least some of those sports at one point.

"Well, when I was little, my mother wasn't exactly the 'sports ball' kind of mom." She makes air quotes with her fingers. "Then when I moved in with Lily, I figured out how clumsy I am. I'm not good at running, doing anything with my hands, and thinking at the same time. You've seen me dance. Just picture that, but add a stick or a projectile of any kind." She shivers. "It's pretty scary."

I laugh. She isn't wrong about her dancing.

We stand there for a moment, looking at the basketball hoop. I can't help but feel a sense of contentment wash over me. Maybe it's the fact that we're doing something together, or maybe it's that there's something about being with her, something almost hypnotic that makes me want to stay with her. I should head inside, but I linger.

"You should join us tomorrow. For pizza night," I blurt out, surprising even myself. "I mean, of course you should join us for dinner. You live here. But usually, on Fridays, Tabby and I get pizza, and we watch a movie. It's a chance for me to catch up with her about school and everything. I thought maybe you might like to join us. For the movie, I mean." I grit my teeth. I swear I was smooth at one point. At least, I thought I was. Maybe not, though. Sonya and I married very young.

She blinks at me, obviously surprised. Perhaps my invitation was unexpected. Usually, if I'm home, June leaves us alone so Tabby and I can spend time together. But I want her to feel like she's welcome, that's all. It's not like this is a date.

"Really?" she asks, her face lighting up. "I'd love to join you guys. It sounds like fun."

Relief floods through me, even though it's really not that big of a deal. It's not like it's an actual date. Still, I can't stop the grin that spreads across my face. "Great. I'll order the pizza. Any preference for toppings?"

"How about we make homemade pizzas?" she offers. "I can make them with whole wheat flour. It'll be healthier. Just tell me what you guys like, and I'll pick it up at the store tomorrow."

"You don't have to—"

She stops me. "I've already told you. I like to cook, and making pizza is fun. We'll do it together."

When she says it like that, with her eyes bright, I believe her. Hanging out with her always seems like fun. "Okay, then. If you're sure."

"I am," she says decisively. "So what movie are we watching?"

I shrug. "Who knows? It's Tabby's turn to pick."

"Ah." She nods. "Should be riveting, then."

I laugh. Together, we pick up the packaging for the hoop and throw it in the trash. I call to Tabby that it's time to come in and get ready for bed, and she hops off the swings and races for the back door.

As we head inside through the garage, though, June pauses in front of me. "Oh, I forgot." She stops so short at the bottom of the stairs that I almost run into her. She spins. "I picked up Tabby…"

Her voice cuts off, though, when she lifts her head to make eye contact.

Only a few inches are between our faces, and I feel as if my body has curled itself around hers. Her eyes widen, and her pupils dilate, and it takes all of my self-discipline to keep from reaching for her. I've never wanted to touch someone so much in my whole life. I try to remember that she's my daughter's nanny, but it's hard to think with her so close. And when her lips part, I want to capture the breath that escapes from them.

The tension between us is so strong I'm not sure I can hold myself steady. I want to touch her, to taste her lips. My body urges me to close the space between us, and I hold myself still to keep from reaching for her.

June doesn't move. She only stands there, staring at me. She's breathing faster, and I can feel her trembling. I'm shaking too. Is she feeling the same need burning through her? Need for contact, for comfort. A raw ache for connection. I have no idea, and I can't ask her. The gap between us stretches wide. I'm her boss, she lives in my home. But also, it's been so long since I've felt anything like this, and I don't trust it. I can't afford to. There's too much on the line.

The moment stretches, and then June steps back. "Oh. Um, I'm sorry." She shifts back from me and glances away, tucking strands of her copper hair behind her ear.

"It's fine." I take a deep breath and try to steady myself. "What was it you were going to say?" I ask, my voice rough as gravel. "About Tabby?"

She waves me off and steps backward up the garage stairs. "You know what? We can chat about it later." She executes a spin on the stairs that's almost graceful. Considering I've seen her dance, it's pretty impressive. She scurries through the door, calling out to Tabby that she needs to tidy up before it's time for her shower, and leaves me standing in my sweltering garage, wondering what the hell just happened.

Whatever it was, I need to make sure it doesn't happen again. I was inches from touching her, from pulling my nanny into my arms and covering her mouth with mine. From blowing everything.

Shaking my head, I follow her inside and do everything I can to tuck my chaotic emotions away where they belong.

June

WHEN DUKE GETS HOME from camp Friday night, he takes in the kitchen. "Are we expecting people?" he asks. As always, he's gorgeous, freshly showered and in sweats after practice. I've been trying to forget the awareness that sparked between us yesterday in the garage. But faced with him alone in the kitchen sends all the heat rushing back.

I do my best to keep it cool. "No," I reply, wiping my hands on the apron I'm wearing. "Why?"

"Daddy!" Tabby comes running into the kitchen and wraps her arms around her father's waist, stepping on the tops of his feet. He walks with her on his feet without missing a beat, and the sight of them takes my breath away. After he deposits a brown bag on the counter, he sweeps his daughter up into his arms and lifts his eyebrows.

"Who's eating all that pizza?" He motions to the balls of dough I've stashed all over the room. "Tabby might have two pieces, and I can't eat all that."

"Pizza makes the best leftovers. Cold pizza for breakfast?" I give a chef kiss. "Perfection."

"It's great, Daddy." Tabby pipes in. "You know I like mine with ranch dressing."

"Wait." I glance wide-eyed between them. "On cold pizza? In the morning? That's... nasty."

"Don't knock it until you try it," Duke says with a shrug, setting his daughter on her feet.

"Pass, guys. Sorry."

"Daddy, it's my turn for the movie this week, right?" Tabby jumps up and down. "You picked last."

"It's your turn. So, what will it be, kid?"

"Frozen."

"The first one?" Duke asks, with a lifted brow.

"The second one isn't good, Dad."

"Fair point," Duke allows, and Tabby bolts off toward the living room. He meets my eyes and rubs the back of his neck. "Is Frozen good for you?"

He holds my gaze, and I almost feel like he's asking me out. Which is ridiculous. But there's a flash of vulnerability on his face, and this version of him—the one that I see sometimes under the gruffness—is kryptonite to me.

It's not only that, though. It's the cozy picture it paints in my head. Curled up on the couch, munching snacks, watching a movie. It's so homey, it makes my heart ache in ways I don't want to poke too hard at. Add the residual heat from yesterday's garage encounter, and I'm off balance.

I clear my throat. "I love Frozen. That Olaf is so handsome."

"The snowman?"

"Obviously." He laughs, and the sound vibrates through me. "Why don't you guys get it set up? We can assemble our pizzas and watch while they're baking."

He nods, heading into the living room after his daughter.

The kitchen looks fine, actually. But I need a moment to gather my professionalism before I join them. Because when I walk into the living room, I need to remember that they're the family here. They hired me to help them. They aren't my family.

Tabby's backpack lies on the floor, and I snag it, just to keep my hands busy. I pull out her lunch box and her water bottle. There's an envelope clipped to the top of her homework folder. It's addressed to the parents and/or guardians of Tabatha York, and I already know what it is.

Since I'm listed as one of her guardians, I open the envelope. Inside, the letter from Miss Shepherd is straightforward. Tabby is a quiet and kind child, but she appears to be struggling. She would like us to fill out the attached form. She says she will follow up with an email and a call if we don't respond.

There are two copies of the Vanderbilt diagnostic scale included behind the letter.

I knew it was coming, but I haven't yet prepared Duke for it. I planned to talk with him about it yesterday in the garage. But when I stopped, it must have caught him off guard because he was too close. Or maybe he wasn't close enough. I looked up in his eyes, and his breath fanned my face, and all I could think about was how his mouth would feel on mine.

His eyes had darkened, and I'm sure he felt something too. But neither of us moved, and the longer the moment dragged out, the more I worried it wasn't desire on his face. I'm his nanny, for heaven's sake, and I was just standing there, gawking at him. By the time I got my wits about me, it didn't seem the right time to bring up my conversation with Miss Shepherd. Neither did the time seem right later in the evening because Duke was exhausted from training camp.

But I don't want to talk about it in front of Tabby. It's hard to say how she would react, and I wasn't sure how he would take the news either. He already knows that something is going on with her, that she's struggling.

I glance toward the living room. We'll talk about it later, when Tabby isn't around to overhear us. Besides, I don't want to interrupt their Friday fun. I can explain everything to him. He loves Tabby, and it's up to him to decide what's best for her. I tuck the Vanderbilt scale on top of the refrigerator.

"Who's ready to put their pizza together?" I call out. There's a cheer from Tabby, and she comes bounding back, her ponytail swaying. My heart twists again.

We'll get her the help she needs. I'm sure of it.

Tabby passes out before Elsa even sings "Let It Go." Duke chuckles and says that's pretty standard for a Friday night. "I can probably count on one hand how many movies Tabby has watched to the end on our movie nights."

He gets up, though, and wraps a blanket around her when she snorts. She's curled in the corner of the sectional.

As the movie hits its climax, I could suggest we turn it off. It's doubtful either of us wants to watch this again. I've seen this movie so many times I can practically recite the lines. But I've got my legs tucked under me next to Tabby, and I'm so comfortable I don't want to move.

At least that's the story I tell myself. Because the reality—that I enjoy sitting next to him like this—is not good. So, I lie to myself, tell myself I'm doing this for him. He's had a long week. I'm only letting him rest.

We don't say anything until the movie's over. In fact, we sit and listen to the music over the end credits. When they're finished, I click it off, and we remain in awkward silence.

"So," I say as he opens his mouth to speak. "Oh, go ahead." We laugh, and he waves me to go ahead instead. "I was just going to say thank you." I grin at him. "This was a lot of fun."

He returns my smile. "My pleasure." He points at his daughter. "I should probably get her upstairs." Tabby's hair is a fuzzy mess, and her mouth is lulling open. "When she sleeps, she looks so much like the toddler I remember."

His face is soft in memory. "You raised her on your own, right?" He tilts his head, and I go on. "I read your wife passed when Tabby was a baby."

He nods. "She did. A brain tumor. She died a couple of months after Tabby was born." He glances away, but not before I see the pain in his features. "I'm sad Tabby didn't get to know her. Sonya would have been a great mom."

"I'm so sorry." I reach over and squeeze his hand. It's not until our skin touches that I realize it might be a mistake.

His hand is warm in mine, and he curls his fingers around my much smaller ones. He glances at our joined hands, and his eyes meet mine. Goose bumps rise on my arms. He swallows, and his gaze falls to my mouth. We're sitting inches apart, and there's an undeniable heat in the air.

I want to kiss him. Or I want him to kiss me. Over the past few days, I've felt the connection between us, and I'm sure he feels it as well. But I can't acknowledge it. Sure, he's my employer, Tabby's father. But more important, he's a serious person, someone who doesn't let people in easily. I want to be part of that inner circle, more than is appropriate, and it scares me. Because at the end of this year, when my contract is over, I'll move on, and so will they.

I can't help how much I admire him, though. He's been through so much. I can't imagine how hard it has been for him. I think about Tabby and the way he loves her. He's an amazing father. But the two of them live here, in this enormous house, alone. My guess is that he and his wife—Sonya—wanted to fill it with children. Life has taken so much away from him.

I let go of his hand, and he looks away. The moment breaks.

"Thank you," he whispers.

Neither of us moves, sitting side by side with his sleeping daughter next to us. I'm sure I should get up and go to bed, but can't force myself to leave him. "You're welcome."

The only sound is Tabby's soft breathing as Duke and I sit in companionable silence. It's strange how it feels to be with him. One moment, I want to throw myself into his arms to see what it feels like to kiss him, to touch him. But times like this? I'm happy to just sit here with him.

I gesture to the movie. "Should we watch it again?"

"I've seen it a million times. I'm sure you know it by heart as well."

"I've seen it a million and one."

He shrugs. "I don't mind watching it again. Or we could watch something else?"

I lift my hands. "It's your movie night, so if you want to watch Frozen, that's cool."

He chuckles, and I am sure neither of us wants to watch Frozen. But I do want to spend more time with him. I shouldn't, but I do. Does he feel the same?

But then he stands, breaking the moment, and stretches his back. I hear his knee pop. He sighs, and it's a weary sound. "I should get Tabby to bed."

I nod, standing as well. "Of course. It's getting late." I tilt my head and glance toward the kitchen. "Before you do, though, I wanted to talk to you about something."

I set aside the blanket I had been using and head for the kitchen, retrieving the envelope from Tabby's teacher from the top of the refrigerator. "I didn't want to talk about this with Tabby in hearing distance, but"—I motion to his daughter, who promptly sleep snorts like a piglet—"I don't think she's listening."

He grins and takes the envelope from me. "No, I don't think so."

I fold my arms over my chest, chewing on my lower lip. His brow furrows as he opens the envelope and reads Miss Shepherd's note.

He holds up the Vanderbilt scale. "What is this?"

"When I picked up Tabby at school yesterday, I spoke with her teacher. She showed me some of the work that Tab has been doing, particularly a writing sample."

"There are writing samples in second grade? Isn't that what they write for college acceptance or something?"

His face has clouded over, and I can tell he's upset, but I keep my voice light. "Anything you write is a writing sample, Duke."

He glances at the note again, still scowling. "Right."

I hurry on. "She's exhibiting some troubling writing patterns. Her teacher would like to refer her to the child study team, but I know for sure that it's easier and faster for the teachers if the parent asks themselves." There's always a lot of red tape in school bureaucracy. When parents get involved, they grease the wheels.

He holds up his hand. "Wait. I'm going to need more explanation. What's a child study team? And what's this form for?"

"That's the Vanderbilt scale. It's usually the first step to determining if classification is required."

"Classification?"

"For special needs resources."

The words fall like bombs between us. "Special needs. Like disability resources?"

I cock my head, nodding. "I suppose it could be. But if we refer Tabby, they'll test her. They'll be able to diagnose any learning disabilities she might have. The sooner we intercede on her behalf, the faster we can get her the tools she needs."

He folds the paper back up and slides it into the envelope. "Do you think she has a learning disability? Is that what this is for?" His voice is sharp, even though he keeps the volume down so he doesn't bother his sleeping daughter. Still, it's an accusation, and I can see he's upset, hurting even. He's lashing out, and my heart aches for him.

"That form is specifically for ADHD, but they'll use it to find out if anyone's witnessing emotional or behavioral challenges."

"What do you mean, anyone else?" He's in full glare mode.

"Her teachers will fill them out and the guidance counselor, anyone who can give additional insight. They'll look at all of them together, see if there's a pattern."

He paces across the room to the window, staring out and giving me his back. I can feel him struggling with his emotions. I don't know him well, but my guess is that his desire to protect Tabby is warring with his desire to do whatever is best. When he speaks, it's a low growl. "Is it... discreet?"

"Discreet?"

"The testing process. Will the other kids in her class know what's going on?" He runs his hands over his hair, and the words hit me like knives. "Will she be embarrassed?" he asks, his voice rough.

I take two steps toward him before I force myself to stop. All I want is to take on some of this burden. Raising Tabby alone after losing his wife, holding his daughter's world together while he does one of the most physically demanding jobs in the world... his strength awes me. When I met him, I thought he was arrogant, full of himself. But now I see he's just guarded and protective.

"No one will know, not unless she tells them."

He nods, and when he turns to face me, his jaw is firm. "Do you believe this is the right thing for her?" The question is soft and genuine.

I swallow to make sure my voice doesn't shake when I answer. "I do."

"Then we can fill this out this weekend, and I'll send whatever email you think I should send to ask for this referral."

I can't stop myself anymore. I step forward, and I wrap my arms around him. He's a mountain, all thick muscles and rangy limbs. He tenses against me, and I think he's going to push me away, but he doesn't. Instead, he folds me against his body. I close my eyes.

He smells amazing, like expensive men's cologne and something evergreen. I allow myself to curve around his body, to sink into the warmth of him. When he speaks, his breath fans my ear. "Thank you."

A shiver races through me, and heat rolls down my spine, like sun-warmed honey. I don't know what he's thanking me for, but we're too close. This is too intimate. I pull back, and he lets me, tucking his hands in his pockets. I look down, anywhere but at him. "Of course. No problem."

He nods, and then he strides toward the couch, scooping his daughter into his arms like she weighs nothing. "Good night, June."

"Good night." I watch him carry her upstairs.

Duke

For the rest of the weekend, I don't allow myself to spend time with June alone, save for the half hour we spend together on Saturday after Tabby goes to bed, filling out the Vanderbilt scales. Even then, I sit across the island from her, and I am careful not to touch her. Like she's a fucking land mine in my house.

If June notices, she says nothing. She's her usual energetic self the entire weekend. Now that the basketball hoop is up, on Sunday afternoon, she tries to show Tabby how to shoot. When it's clear she is as bad at basketball as she is at dancing, I take over. Before long, Tabby tosses the ball in the hoop easily from the lowest setting, and I crank the apparatus to lift the basket a couple feet.

As I guide Tabby's hands to hold the basketball, I notice June watching us. Her face is soft.

My body tightens as I think of holding her on Friday night, remembering the feel of her pressed against me. She fit there, but it was more than that. She wanted to comfort me. I tilted my head into the curve of her neck, and her scent was irresistible. A few more moments, and I would have pressed my lips on that skin. I was seconds from tasting her.

But she pulled back, stepped away. She saved us. I should have been strong enough to do it, but I hadn't been. With June, the temptation is too much.

Shaken by my thoughts, I fumble the ball, and it bounces off my hands, rolling to a stop at her feet. She bends over to pick it up, giving me a clear view of the skin on her collarbone. I look away, even as my fingers itch with the need to touch her.

Her face reddens, and she stands. Does she know what I'm thinking? I swear, I have more discipline than this.

"I'm going to go in and make dinner," she says, jutting a thumb toward the kitchen. She doesn't wait for a response, only retreats inside, leaving me with Tabby.

"What's wrong with June?" Tabby asks, taking the ball from me.

"Nothing, baby girl." It's not June with the problem right now. It's me. "Let's try some dribbling."

I keep Tabby outside until June calls us for dinner. We put the ball away in the garage and then wash our hands in the powder room.

The second I step into the kitchen, I'm struck again at the changes she's made to my home. The house has never been this tidy. Mrs. Reyes cleans, but during the times she's not there, Tabby and I aren't exactly neat. We throw our trash out and put our clothes in the laundry baskets, but it's the bare minimum. As a single parent and professional athlete, I'm crazy busy. But this week has been different.

The house isn't just tidy—it's homey. There's always music on. June brought flowers from somewhere. Not the kind I could buy at the florist or grocery store, but the kind that grow somewhere. She probably picked them herself. And the baking. There have been so many muffins and baked goods that have gone through my kitchen, I'm going to need to say something. I can't eat like this all the time without dragging ass on the rink. But I haven't got the heart to tell her to stop.

Hell, who am I kidding? The shit she makes is amazing, and I've liked it all so much. I don't want her to stop. Though I might need to ask her to have a consideration for my scale and for Coach Hargreeves's sanity.

As we sit down to eat, June brings out a new dish. It appears to be some kind of casserole, but I can't really tell what's in it. It looks like mostly vegetables. Maybe sausage? I take a bite, and it's like heaven in my mouth. I can feel my eyes roll back in pleasure.

"What is this?" I ask between bites.

"It's sausage and peppers, but I added beans and stuff because the dietician says complex fiber is good for you."

Tabby pushes around pieces of sausage on her plate. "Beans make me toot, so June said I could just have the sausage."

"Tab," I warn.

"What?" she asks as she spears another sausage medallion. "That's what you always tell me."

I sigh as June smothers a laugh. "Right. I do. Thank you, though, June. This is great." She nods, blushing, and I shift in my seat. No one has ever made me this hot with their blushes. I shake my head and refocus on my dinner. I can't keep thinking about her like this.

After dinner, I volunteer to do the dishes while June takes Tabby upstairs to get ready for bed. As I scrub a pot, I hear the stairs creak and look up to see June standing there.

"Hey," she says, leaning against the door frame.

"Hey." I try to keep it cool, but with her, I don't think I have it in me. I direct all my attention to the dishes, burying my hands in the soapy water. Having June cook is great, but she uses a lot more dishes than I do with the stuff I make.

"Listen, Duke..." I don't look at her, but I can feel her shuffling closer to me. I keep my back turned because I know looking at her only makes everything harder. "Um... I wanted to say I'm sorry."

At that, I do glance over my shoulder. "Sorry?" Not what I expected.

She folds her arms over her chest, and everything in her stance suggests discomfort. But that's something I admire about her. Even if something's awkward, she still powers through. "I'm sorry I hugged you the other night. In the living room. After Frozen. I shouldn't have done that."

I reach for the kitchen towel and dry my hands, buying myself time to think. She regrets hugging me. I'm surprised at how much that bothers me. No... it's not that it bothers me. It feels wrong. I wanted that hug. The same as I want to talk to her, learn more about her. I want...

I want her. I want to kiss her. I want to touch her and lose myself in the feel of her skin. I want to bury myself in her until we're both drowning in the pleasure of one another. It's hard to understand how I could feel all of those things if she isn't feeling any of them.

Then again, even if she did, it's not my place to pursue it. I want us to be friends, to work together like she suggested, but I need to keep the balance. I need to maintain the boundaries.

"It's no big deal at all," I offer, trying to keep my voice breezy. "We're friends. Friends hug."

She nods, and I see her swallow. Her face rearranges into nonchalance. "Right. Exactly." She shrugs, waving it off. "I just... after all the stuff at the interview, about personal relationships... I didn't want you to think I was coming on to you or something."

Of course, she's worrying about that. When I told Raybourne I needed to avoid any drama or scandals this year, I never expected I would be the one putting myself in that kind of jeopardy. Last year, a defenseman had an affair with a woman in marketing. The whole mess ended up in his nasty divorce and custody battle. It felt important to mention a need for professionalism in my interview process.

"Absolutely not." I give her my most confident grin. "We're friends. All good."

"Right." She rocks back and forth on her heels. Pointing to the stairs, she inches that way, all smiles. "Great then. I'll just run up and make sure Tabby's moving along."

"Sounds good." I force myself to go back to the dishes, like holding her meant nothing to me. Like I feel nothing at all.

Out of the corner of my eye, I watch her go and then close my eyes, sucking in breaths that do nothing to slow my heart. This whole situation is supposed to have made my life easier. I have no idea how I've lost control of everything.

June

WE DECIDE ON A Saturday evening for the barbecue because the team is off Sunday. I want to make some of the food, but Duke insists we cater. I agree but draw the line at desserts. They're my specialty. Since we were talking about it over text, I think he tires of arguing with me and gives in.

I don't know any caterers in Haddonfield, but Moorestown is close enough. On Tuesday, I contact the local delicatessen there. Marie, the owner's wife, takes my call. "Oh, Miss June! It's so nice to hear from you. How is Lily?"

Marie and Lily went to school together. We used to walk to Marie and Luca's deli on Sundays to buy snacks. Lily had limited extra money, but she said Sundays were special. She let us pick out something sweet while she caught up with Marie.

"She's claustrophobic, living in a small apartment. You know how she is. She needs space to roam."

Marie chuckles. "That she does. What can I do for you?"

I explain what I'll need for the barbecue, and Marie has suggestions. We agree on a menu, and she offers to deliver the food, but I decline. Marie and Luca aren't young anymore, so they hire out for delivery. It's not a big deal for me to get it. In the garage, the Range Rover is sitting there, not being used. I can use it for this.

The second week of training is more intense than the first, so I hardly see Duke at all. He leaves before six and comes home after dinner most nights. Though she misses her father, Tabby doesn't seem phased by the change. This isn't her first rodeo, I guess. But I can see now why having a live-in caretaker makes sense to them. To keep her mind off missing her dad, I enlist her to help organize the barbecue. When I suggest we decorate the backyard, Tabby isn't enthusiastic, so I keep it simple. But she gets excited about the karaoke machine. I bring it up as a joke, but she is immediately on board. I text Duke, thinking he'll put a stop to the idea, but he surprises me, too. So, Saturday morning, someone Duke's hired sets up a karaoke machine under the rented tent out by the pool.

I pick up the food, and by mid-afternoon, we're set. There's pulled pork, sausage and peppers, roast beef, and a bunch of vegetables and salads. I tried to keep in mind the guys' diet as much as I could. For the kids, we've got macaroni and cheese and hot dogs. We rented an ice cream machine, too, since it's going to be a hot day. I figure the kids will be in and out of the pool, so they can cool off if they're hot.

After Duke's morning practice, he gets home as Tabby and I are putting together cookie trays. "Whoa," he says. "You said you'd keep it simple for dessert."

"This is simple. It's cookies." I survey the counters. Tabby and I made three different types this week—chocolate chip, white chocolate macadamia nut, and snickerdoodles. Yesterday, we worried that wouldn't be enough, so we made brownies and blondies too.

"Didn't you rent an ice cream machine too?"

"Yes."

The doorbell rings, and he laughs. "Your definition of simple and mine are not the same." He wanders off to answer the door. I glance at Tabby.

"Do you think it's too much?" I ask.

She shrugs. "I'm seven. Looks good to me." She hops off the stool and heads into the foyer, probably to see if anyone her age is here. Quickly, I wash my hands and take a deep breath, staunching anxiety. There's no reason to be nervous, after all. This isn't my house or my party, at least not really. Still, I want everyone to have a good time, and I want Duke to be pleased he let me coordinate it.

Mostly, I'm excited to spend some time with him, even if I plan to stay mostly in the background, making sure things run smoothly.

Though I told myself I was trying to keep Tabby busy so she wouldn't miss her father, I missed Duke too. We've been busy. Besides baking cookies with Tabby, I've been working with her on her writing. She's struggling, and she hates it, so we take a lot of breaks. I sent in the Vanderbilt scales on Monday, but I don't know how long it'll be until we get the results.

During the days, I took Lily to dialysis three times this week. There's not much to do there, so I stopped at the thrift store Tuesday and got us some new books—romance for her, some new science fiction for me. I already finished one and left it on Duke's desk in case he wanted to try it. Because we're friends and friends share books.

My problem is that I haven't been thinking of him as a friend at all this week.

I shake my head and plant a smile on my face to greet the first guests to arrive.

Duke is talking as he walks into the kitchen with an enormous man and a beautiful blonde. "I'd like you to meet June. This entire party was her idea," he offers, and I beam. Then he adds, "She's Tabby's nanny."

The words bother me. I don't know why—they're true. But sometime this week, I stopped focusing on that role and started seeing myself differently. Like I'm more important than that, somehow. Though what could be more important than the person who takes care of his daughter? Nanny is exactly what I am. I need to keep that in the forefront of my mind.

I hold my hand out to the newcomers, doing my best to keep my face bright. "Hi. Thanks for coming."

"This is Hunter Mason," Duke offers. I mustn't have hidden my reaction well, because he gives me a questioning glance. "And his girlfriend, Violet."

"Not his girlfriend," Violet adds, folding my hand in both of hers. I catch the softest hint of a Southern or Midwestern accent, but I can't place it. "Friends. Hunter and I went to college together in Chesterboro. He's been showing me around since I moved here." When she grins at me, it's warm and welcoming. Violet is gorgeous, tall with blond hair, and she radiates confidence.

"You know that's not true," Hunter adds. His voice is calm and firm as he shakes my hand. Hunter seems to be Violet's opposite. Quiet, reserved. In dark-framed glasses, he has a serious, unreadable face.

She waves a hand at him, making the movement look sophisticated and breezy. "You're right. I'm lying. I've been dragging him out every chance I can get. So many fun restaurants and bars in Philadelphia, such interesting culture here. After Chesterboro, I've been dying to soak it up. Hunter is my begrudging plus-one."

"Not begrudging," he says, pushing his glasses up on his nose. He shifts his weight, and though he's a giant, taller than Duke even and just as muscular, he strikes me as shy.

The doorbell rings again, and Duke motions to the backyard. "Food's out. Help yourself," he offers before heading for the entrance again. Hunter follows his cue.

Violet hangs back. "I'll be right there, Hunt," she calls. "Did you need any help?" she asks me. Under her breath, she adds. "Are you okay?"

"Of course," I offer. "I'm so happy to have everyone here. Why?"

Violet's gaze lingers on me for a moment longer before she nods. "Okay. Good. For a second there, you just looked... Oh, I don't know. I'm silly." She waves off whatever she was going to say. "Did you need help, though? Do you want me to carry anything outside?"

"That would be great. I set up a dessert table."

"As opposed to this?" She opens her arms. "This is a dessert kitchen." I laugh, and she adds. "These all look delicious, by the way. Where did you get them?"

"Tabby—Duke's daughter—and I made them."

"You made these all? Wow." She glances around. "Mind if I snag one?"

"We're adults, right?" I pick up one of the white chocolate macadamia nut cookies. I make them with coconut, and they're my favorites. "We can eat dessert first if we want." I bite into it and sigh. Chewy and sweet, just right.

Violet laughs, and it's a charming, musical sound. She picks up a chocolate chip cookie and sinks her teeth in. After she finishes chewing, she points at me with the rest of the cookie. "This is heaven.

And you are a girl after my heart. I think we are going to be good friends." She pops the rest into her mouth, winking at me.

I can't help but smile. We each pick up two platters of treats, and Violet follows me outside. Duke must have had people file in through the side gate because the place was filling up. Violet and I put the cookies down. She motions to the corner, mischief in her eyes. "Wait. Is that a karaoke machine?"

I laugh. Violet's right. I think we could be good friends. "It is."

She grabs my hand. "Do you have anything else to do? For the party, I mean."

I glance around. People are standing, sipping lemonade and having appetizers. "I don't think…"

She drags me toward the stage. "Do you sing?"

"I mean, anyone can sing," I offer.

"I was in pageants as a girl." She waves this off like it doesn't matter at all, but I can picture Violet as a beauty queen. "Lots of nonsense, but I love to sing. Come up with me?"

"Um…"

"It'll be fun." She's so convincing, and isn't that the reason we rented the thing, anyway? Besides, if other people see us using it, maybe they'll join in. The more fun everyone has, the better for team bonding.

"Sure. Why not? But I'm awful."

"I'm sure you'll be great," she assures me.

"Don't say I didn't warn you."

Duke

"You need to save her." Huck motions to the corner of the tent, where Violet and June are singing the words to "Living on a Prayer." Rather, June is warbling happily off-key, and Violet is trying to sing. Violet has stuck a finger in the ear closest to June, probably to tune her out. She's increased her volume a couple times and keeps casting glances at June, as if wondering if it's possible for someone to be so cluelessly out of tune.

I chuckle. "Save June? Or Violet?"

Huck sips a light beer, considering. "Violet looks like she's having a rougher time."

Next to us, Hunter has a plate of appetizers—vegetables and dip, some cheese, and lean meats—and he's scarfing it all down. "Violet's fine. She probably dragged June up there. She's really convincing. Like a politician."

I study them. "Neither of them looks unhappy. I say we let it play out." It's true. Though Violet looks confused, maybe even impressed by June's inability to carry a tune, she doesn't look uncomfortable. For her part, June is happily belting out the Jon Bon Jovi song like she's singing alone in the car.

"What about the rest of us?" Hunter pauses, casting me an assessing stare. "I see. You're a real sadist, aren't you?"

I grunt. "You've been on my runs."

He nods, going back to his food. "Truth."

Over the past two weeks, I've come to like the kid. Hunter's only twenty-two, and he spent four years as a winger at Chesterboro. He wasn't one of their flashier players, but he works hard, he's fast, and he plays scrappy if he needs to. He came into camp as a long shot to make the opening day roster, but I'm thinking he just might stick instead of being sent down to the minors. His personality meshes with what we're trying to do here in Philadelphia. Do your job, no drama.

The song continues, and June crones along with it. The notes are off-key. Sometimes, she hits the wrong note or lingers too long on another. Violet carries them across the finish line.

At the end, I clap, but I think I'm the only one. With a pacifying smile, Violet whispers something to June before taking the microphone from her and handing it to a pair of middle school girls. An upbeat pop melody spills from the speakers as Violet and June head toward us. The preteens break out into the lyrics, and even they're better than June and Violet managed.

"We should do another one," June says, her eyes shining when she reaches the table.

"Oh, absolutely," Violet responds. "But I wanted to, um, get Hunter to sing with me first." She tugs on Hunter's arm, and his eyes get as big as saucers behind his glasses. "Come on, Hunt. Let's go pick out a song."

"Vi…" Hunter's face is a mask of horror.

"Maybe later?" June calls after them, all hopeful anticipation.

"Definitely." Violet says, dragging Hunter behind her. "Later." She pulls him toward the karaoke book, Hunter clearly trying to stall.

June chuckles, and we meet each other's gaze. "You have no intention of singing again, do you?" I ask her, barely containing my amusement.

"No way. You heard me. I'm awful." Next to me, Huck busts up laughing, and she grins at him. "I'm June Harlow, by the way."

"I know," Huck says. "You're Tabby's nanny. I'm Huck Sokolov."

"It's nice to meet you." She glances in front of him. "Did you get something to eat?"

"I had some snacks. I'm going to get a sandwich soon."

"Dessert?"

"Not yet, but I'm stuffed."

She nods in approval, glances around. "Good. I'm going to check on everyone else and make sure Tabby put on sunscreen." She meets my gaze, and I'm caught again by the connection between us. "Do you need anything?"

The words are innocent, but they send desire coursing through me. The past week has been a lesson in unrequited need. I'm always aware of where she is in my home. I listen for her laughs, eager for them. My time at the rink should give me some relief, but it doesn't. I catch myself thinking about her constantly, the way she ruffles Tabby's hair, the way she listens intently to the answers to our questions. I've become addicted to her—her smile, the way she moves, the way she sees me.

I shake my head. "I'm good. Thank you."

She nods. "Nice to meet you, Huck." She waves, leaving us alone at the table. I watch her walk away, admiring the way the sundress hangs on her lithe frame.

There's a long pause, and Huck finally exhales a heavy breath. "You're fucked, aren't you?"

I sigh, glancing again at June, who's at the food tables, checking everything. "It seems so."

The punch he gives me stings. "You're a goddamned moron."

"Agreed."

"You're never home, dumbass. How hard is it to stay away from someone you hardly ever see?"

I narrow my eyes at him. "I am staying away from her." All I've done is stay away from her for the past two weeks. It's maddening.

Huck leans closer. "That's not what staying away from someone looks like."

Across the tent, June's chatting with Travis Lancaster and Colt Carmichael. I see the looks on their faces. That's what interest looks like. Every instinct in me screams to get up, to intercede. But why? It's not inappropriate for her to get to know them, even to date one of them if she wanted. She's not living under their roof, and they aren't paying her salary.

I grit my teeth, and my hold on my beer bottle tightens.

"She seems pretty amazing," Huck says. My gaze finds his, and I glare at him. He lifts his hands. "I know. Hands off." He chuckles. "I'm no threat, trust me. I have my own stuff. But it's true. You know it is. She's smart, funny, it seems. She planned this entire party for our team. And Barnett said she made the cookies herself?" I nod. He whistles under his breath. "I take it back then. Maybe I should propose."

Whatever he sees on my face makes him bark out a laugh. I can only glare at him. He's right—she is amazing. Sharp-witted and funny, a natural caretaker. Not just for Tabby, but for everyone. She's been taking her foster mother to dialysis all week. When I asked, she said Lily argued with her about it, and said she could take public transportation. But June wouldn't hear it, and my guess is that Lily didn't mean it, anyway. I would always choose time with June versus time alone, too.

But it's not only things like that. She is constantly doing small things for everyone, just random acts of kindness. I found a book on my desk with a Post-it, saying she thought I would like it. She made me overnight oats, throwing in strawberries and raspberries because she noticed I enjoyed them.

It's nearly impossible not to fall in love with her.

I jolt, wondering where the hell that thought came from. I shake my head. Falling in love is not what I need right now. I need to focus on hockey, on leading this team.

Huck leans back in his chair, studying me. "You know, if you don't make a move soon, someone else will. She's hot as hell."

I glare at him. "That's not the point."

He shrugs. "Whatever you say, man. But you've got to see that everyone else notices, too."

I do see that. My teammates obviously notice anyway. Every time I look at her, one of them is chatting her up. But I can't just make a move. All the professional reasons aside, what if she doesn't feel the same way? Then everything will be awkward. No, June is off limits. She's Tabby's nanny and under my care.

But as I watch her laugh with Travis and Colt, I can't help thinking I'm not in control of my feelings anymore.

Every hour I spend around June, my resolve to steer clear of her crumbles a little more. It's only a matter of time before I'm left with only one option. And that terrifies the hell out of me.

June

THE BARBECUE GOES OFF without a hitch. Well, mostly anyway. There's plenty of food, and everyone raves over my desserts. There aren't that many kids who come, but the handful that are there spend the afternoon in the pool or covered in melting ice cream. The karaoke machine is an enormous hit. After Violet and I get it started, it feels like everyone sings something. Tabby even convinces Duke to sing with her. He harmonizes along with her to a song by Taylor Swift, Tabby's favorite.

Everybody heads out by dusk, some of them joking with Duke about how they're exhausted because their captain is a dick and forces early morning runs. He doesn't react much to the teasing, but I can tell he's pleased. Violet and Hunter hang around at the end because Violet insists on helping me clean up, claiming it reminds her of how they cleaned up after sorority parties in college. Then she throws her arms around me in a hug and insists we get together for lunch or something soon. I quickly agree.

Duke takes Tabby up for her bath while I store the leftovers and start in on the dishes. They come down so Tabby can hug me good night before he takes her back up to tuck her in. When he rejoins me, he falls into the cleanup in companionable silence.

I've already done the hard stuff. By the time he finishes loading the dishwasher, there are only a couple of pots and serving platters left. He steps up to the sink, so I grab a hand towel and wait to dry.

"Thank you so much," he offers, his hands buried in soapy water. "Between the planning, the decorating, the desserts... You did a great job."

Pleasure sings through me as I take the first pot from him. "You're welcome. It looked like everyone had a good time. What do you think?" I spent a lot of time running around, but it seemed like everyone was getting along. "It was a lot of fun getting to plan with Tabby. I think she had fun, too, in the pool. So that's good too."

"Everyone had fun. I'm sure of that. I saw some of the older guys chatting with the younger ones. We have a split locker room, veterans and newbies. Today, they were mingling." He hands me a platter. "I couldn't figure out how to bridge that gap. But you did. Thank you."

I dry the serving platter and set it on the island, emotion welling in my chest. The intensity of his words makes me uncomfortable, so I try to smooth over the awkwardness. "Of course. You're welcome. We're friends, after all." As I turn to face him, I notice how close we're standing. I can feel his breath on my cheek and his eyes lock on to mine. "Friends."

The last word comes out as a whisper, and I search his face. He sets the hand towel he just used to dry his hand on the island behind me, closing the distance between us. I can hardly breathe.

He looks down at me, his gaze conflicted. Electricity runs through me, heating me. His eyes flicker to my lips for a moment before he speaks. "We are," he agrees, his voice low and husky. "Friends."

We stare at each other. The only thing between us is the sound of our breathing, fast, erratic. My heart races in my chest. My skin feels too sensitive, and maybe that's why the piece of hair that's come out of my braid tickles my cheek so much. With a quick swipe, I brush it back from my face, dropping my hand to my side again.

He follows the movement, and we both watch as he takes my hand. The feel of his warm fingers on my skin is intoxicating. His grip is firm but not painfully so, and he rubs his thumb across my knuckles, sending a shiver through me.

"But June?" he whispers.

I swallow hard, my eyes locked with his. "Yeah?" I reply, my voice barely audible. His touch is doing things to me I can't quite explain. I feel vulnerable, yet I want to lean closer.

"I can't stop thinking about you. Not like friends." His voice is raw, his eyes searching mine as if looking for some sort of answer. He closes the distance between us, his free hand moving to my waist, pulling me gently toward him. Our bodies are so close that I can feel the warmth of him. "I want to kiss you, June," he murmurs, his voice low and husky.

My heartbeat picks up. I know it's wrong to feel this way, especially since this is Duke, but I can't help it. I want to kiss him too.

My body presses against him. I can feel his breath on my lips, his hand still holding mine as his other hand grips my waist. It's like the air is thick with desire, and I can't resist any longer.

I don't know if he leans toward me, or if I lean toward him. It's both, it seems, because our mouths meet in the center. The kiss begins as a gentle exploration, yet quickly becomes heated. His hands move from my waist to my back, pulling me closer as his tongue finds mine. I melt against him and grip his shirt, feeling the powerful muscles of his chest beneath my fingers. He deepens the kiss, and I feel something inside me awaken. His hands move up, cradling my face as his fingers tangle in my hair. His touch is gentle yet demanding, and I can't help but respond to him with a moan of pleasure.

I'm completely lost in the moment, and all thoughts of what's wrong or right, that he's my boss, whatever... all of it fades away. All that matters is the way his lips move against mine and the warmth of his hands on my skin. When we break apart, my breath comes in shallow gasps, and I take a few moments to remember where we are.

Duke rests his forehead against mine, panting. His eyes fill with cloudy desire and conflict. Taking a step back, he releases my hand and runs one of his through his dark hair.

"Shit," he murmurs, looking away from me. "I shouldn't have done that."

My heart races, and I'm unsure of what to say. The kiss was amazing, and I can't deny that I want more, but it's not that simple.

"It's okay," I finally say, my voice barely above a whisper. "It was just a kiss." The words are knives in my stomach. It wasn't just a kiss—it was one of the most erotic experiences in my life.

Duke looks back at me, his eyes scanning my face before he nods in agreement. "We shouldn't have done that. It was a mistake."

The words sting. He's right, of course. It was a mistake. A perfect, hot mistake.

Duke takes a step to the side, putting more distance between us. "We'll just forget this ever happened."

"Exactly. Like nothing ever happened." The thought of forgetting is painful, but it would be too risky to do anything else. This is already too close to disaster. Tabby needs me. Besides, where could this even go—kissing my boss? We can't have a personal relationship, not if he's paying me. And how would we explain that to Tabby? Add in the lack of professionalism, and it's uncalled for.

I should have never let things get to this point. I take a deep breath and nod again.

"I'm sorry, June. I really am," he says. With a nod, Duke grabs his things and heads upstairs, leaving me alone in the kitchen. I stand there for a few moments, still feeling the warmth of his lips on mine.

He's right. That can't happen again. That kiss—the best kiss of my life—was a complete mistake. From here forward, I need to step back from Duke York. If this is what friendship with him looks like, it's too dangerous.

As promised, Duke pretends like the kiss we shared never happened, and so do I. The next week, Duke is at the rink from dawn until dusk. I drive Lily to her dialysis and help Tabby with her homework. Technically, things are the same. But when Duke and I are together, there's a new tension between us. We're too formal, constantly on guard.

I hate it, but it's better this way. That's what I keep telling myself. Because if I relax, I'm afraid I'll slip. I'll get too close, touch him when I shouldn't. It'll be an accident, or I won't be expecting it, but it'll be devastating. Right now, I've braced myself.

I miss him, though. I see him the same amount as before, but I miss him.

A week after our kiss, we visit Lily's kidney doctor, Dr. Jones, before her dialysis. He pushes a folder across the desk to us. "Your body isn't reacting to the treatments as we hoped," he tells her. "We originally believed your kidneys were functioning at about fifteen percent, but we now know it's lower."

"What does that mean?" I ask.

"Lily is retaining water and toxins in her blood. We're going to adjust her dialysis accordingly." He inhales. "However, that's a short-term solution. Our team believes the only true long-term solution for her is a transplant. We've already started the paperwork, but I must warn you the demand is great, and Lily has preexisting conditions that could complicate her status on the transplant list."

"Long-term?" I'm stopped up on that point. I glance back and forth between him and Lily.

Lily sighs. "He means the dialysis won't keep me alive for long, and if I don't get a transplant soon, I'll die." She's never been one to shy away from a truth. As a foster mother, she's witnessed too many difficult situations. She always says it's best to just get on with it.

My eyes widen. "But you only started dialysis." At our first appointments, they assured us Lily could live for ten or more years on dialysis.

"Lily's situation is in constant fluctuation," Dr. Jones says. "We believe her diabetes and blood pressure are under control now, but the effects of the past six months on her body are significant."

"I see." I do. I hate it, but I get it.

He motions to the paperwork in front of me. "Let's go over these numbers, and they should give you a better understanding of where we are." What follows is fifteen minutes of medical explanation, but all of it adds up to the original assessment. Lily needs a new kidney, and she doesn't have a lot of time to wait for it.

"Well, can't you survive with only one kidney?" I ask when he's finished.

"Yes. But neither of Lily's work right now."

"I have two. I'll give her one of mine." This seems like an easy fix. "I'm healthy. I mean, I think I am. I'll have whatever tests done that you need. But if Lily could use one of my kidneys, she's welcome to it."

"June—" Lily's already closed her eyes, shaking her head.

Dr. Jones cuts her off. "It's not as easy as just letting anyone on the street give someone a kidney, Miss Harlow," he cautions, but he reaches into a cabinet next to him. Retrieving a pamphlet, he slides it across the desk to me. "This will give you some information about the procedure and what to expect if you decide to proceed with testing."

I nod, taking the booklet. "I'm already sure I'd like to go through the testing."

"June," Lily's tone is sharp, but I raise my hand to stop her.

"There's no harm in testing. If I'm a match for you, then we can make final decisions." Even the cursory scan of the paperwork shows the testing process is extensive, but I'm willing to do whatever it takes. "Thank you, Dr. Jones," I say, determinedly. "Could you email me the forms I need to fill out to start the process?"

He looks between Lily and me. I don't know what he sees, but he nods. "Elaine, at the nurses' station, can help you with that."

We shake his hand and leave his office. We aren't even in the hall when Lily snags my sleeve and stops me.

"I can't let you do this." She's got the stubborn tilt to her chin. I'm familiar with that look. It means she's about to give me hell. "I'm an old woman. You are a young woman. I'm not a good place to put one of your perfectly healthy kidneys."

"First, you're not old. Sixty-two is still young." I hold up a finger, counting off. "And second, you're right. I'm a grown woman, and if I want to get tested to find out if my kidney matches my mother, then that's what I can do." I lift my hand when she protests. "And you're my mother in every way that's important."

Her eyes soften. "I know, girl. But I don't want to put you through that kind of risk. You have your whole life ahead of you."

"I won't let you just give up, Lily. You raised me to be strong, remember?" I take her arm and start walking down the hallway again. "Besides, it's not like I'm doing this on my own. I'll have the doctors and nurses guiding me through the entire process. And if it turns out I'm not a match, then at least we tried." I pull her into a brief hug. "I want to do this for you, Lily. You've done so much for me. You didn't just take me in, you raised me, loved me, and gave me a home. Now it's my turn to give back to you."

Tears fill her eyes. "I don't want you risking your health for me."

"I'm not risking anything. I already told you that. There are lots of people who donate kidneys to their loved ones. And you are loved by me. So let me at least look into it."

She scans my face. "You're sure about this?"

I nod, looping my arm through hers. "I'm sure."

"What about your job? What about Duke and Tabby?"

"I don't know. But as you said, that's a job. You're my family." I give her hand a squeeze. "Let's just see what happens with the testing, okay?"

Lily nods, still hesitant, but I can see the hope in her eyes as she heads off to get hooked up to her dialysis machine. I make my way to the nurses' station. Maybe this is the solution, the way she can live longer, see me grow old, maybe even have children of my own someday. I'll do whatever it takes to help Lily.

At the nurses' station, I find out there's a payment due for her treatments and that she's not even close to meeting her insurance's high deductible. I use my debit card and empty my bank account. When I sit down with Lily, I ask as gently as I can if she has any savings left. She admits she doesn't but suggests that it's time to consider selling some things from her storage. I argue, trying to think of any other way to avoid selling her prized possessions. But we both know there isn't. Lily only accepts the truth faster. She not only has medical bills but needs to cover the costs of home ownership and everyday life.

We make a list of items she's prepared to part with. She gives suggestions of their value, and the entire process hurts my heart. I mention that based on the paperwork, the cost of a kidney transplant might save money in the long run. Lily swallows that news like she's drinking poison.

By the time I pull into the driveway at home, I'm mentally exhausted. Maybe that's why I don't immediately register the construction van there.

Unsure of what's going on, I text Duke. *There's a handyperson here. Is that on purpose?* He hadn't told me about any scheduled work.

Yes. I hoped they'd be gone by the time you got back.

Is everything okay?

Yes. Tell me how it looks.

Since there's no danger, I head inside and follow the sounds of construction upstairs. It's coming from the playroom. I knock on the doorjamb as I step in, not wanting to surprise anyone holding power tools. "Hello?"

Inside, though, I pause, gasping.

Someone has completely covered the walls with bookshelves. The wood is bare—cherry or maple, maybe—but the structures are in place. Since the playroom has high ceilings, the amount of shelf space is significant. "Oh," I sigh out.

An older man holds a nail gun on a ladder, and a younger man kneels on the ground amidst a lot of raw lumber. The older man smiles when he sees me. "You must be Miss Harlow."

"I am."

"I hope we're not disturbing you too much," the older man says apologetically. "We're just finishing up the last touches. I'm Dave, and that's my son, Mike."

"What is this?"

The younger man stands up and brushes off his pants. "Duke wanted it to be a surprise."

"A surprise?" I ask, turning to face him.

Dave nods. "He called us last week, said he wanted to turn the playroom into a library."

I walk around the room, running my hand over the smooth wood of the shelves. "It's perfect," I say. "But... why?"

The younger man smiles. "He said you and Tabby love to read. And he wants to make sure you have a place to do that. He wanted it done before the furniture arrives."

"Furniture?" There's already a loveseat in here and a desk with a chair.

"He ordered three oversized chairs. Said that no one needs this desk any longer, so we'll move that out when we go."

I spin around in the center of the room. "It's beautiful. Thank you."

Dave chuckles. "You don't have to thank us. We just do the work. Your man is paying the bills."

I shake my head. "Oh, he's not my—" I stop myself. What is Duke? He's my boss, and we're supposed to be friends. But I need to admit how much more he is than that. He's important to me. Not just because he's Tabby's father, and I love the little girl. I care for him too.

As I stand there, staring at the beautiful shelves, I realize Duke has been paying attention. He's noticed what I love and what I need. I'm not the only one feeling more than professionalism. Duke has made this room for me, for us, and it's not just because Tabby and I love to read. I can feel his presence in the room, even though he's not here.

"Thank you," I murmur again, feeling tears prick at the corners of my eyes. "This is amazing."

Dave nods, and Mike grins at me. "Glad you like it. All we have left to do is the ladder." He motions to the ground and the lumber scattered there.

"Ladder?"

He motions to a rail attached across the top of the shelves. "Duke said if you and Tabby are going to have a fairy tale library, it needs to have a ladder you can swing from, like princesses in the movies."

I snort, then I crack up. As Dave and Mike stare at me like I've lost my mind, I laugh and laugh. This is exactly what I needed after the long morning I had. Waving my hand, I gasp out, "I'm sorry. Excuse me. I'll get out of your way."

I make my way from the room, wiping the tears of laughter from my eyes. But it's impossible to ignore the gooey feelings in my chest.

Did Duke know how much this would mean to me? It's not just the shelves or the chairs or the ladder. It's the fact he listened to me, paid attention to what I love, and did something special.

Yes, things are complicated, but I can't keep lying to myself. I care about him more than I should and more than I want to. He's right—we can't let anything physical happen between us, especially now. If Lily needs me, and I end up having this surgery for her, I don't know how long the recovery time is or what that means for my time with Duke and Tabby. Even considering that I might need to leave them makes my stomach twist.

That's just adding trouble to an already complex situation. I don't want to think about it. Right now, all I want to think about is that a wonderful man built Tabby and me a library. I'm not sure I can resist falling in love with a man like that.

Duke

Training camp is the same as it is every year—too short, but also too fucking long. There's not enough time for us to gel properly, but by the time we get to the season opener, we're all champing at the bit to play an actual game. We have preseason showdowns, but everyone knows they aren't as competitive. The atmosphere in the stands isn't the same either.

So, I breathe a sigh of relief when I park outside the stadium for our first game. As I step out of the car, adrenaline hits my veins. The air is electric, filled with the excited chatter of fans as they stream inside. I make my way to the locker room, feeling the familiar sense of purpose.

My teammates are already getting ready. Everyone prepares for a game differently. Some of them joke around to blow off steam while others remain focused and silent. I give everyone the space to do their own thing, keeping watch on the newbies to make sure they're solid. Already dressed and ready, Travis Lancaster taps his heels on the ground, his knee bouncing as he looks at something in front of him. I don't see anything there, but whatever. He looks ready, so I leave him to his vacant staring.

The coaches come in, giving us last-minute instructions and pep talks. I listen intently. This is almost certainly my last first game, and

I need to start the season as I plan to go on. It's my last chance to shine, to show the world what I'm capable of.

We cycle through our warm-ups, and when we return to the locker room, Hargreeves gives his last give-'em-hell speech before we head back out to the ice.

As we step out onto the ice, the crowd roars. The sound of their excitement rattles through me. This is what I live for, and energy courses through me. We stretch our legs, skating around the rink, before we head to blue lines for the national anthems.

The house lights dim, and our singer steps onto the ice. She does a great job, as always. But though I have respect for both Canada and the United States, I can never stand still before games. I shift, shuffling my feet on the blue line, barely making out any of the words as she drones on.

That's when I glance across the rink and see June.

She and Tabby are in the family section, both of them wearing jerseys with my number. June is rocking back and forth as she chews on her thumbnail. Her anxiety wafts across the ice to me, hitting me in the center of the chest. She's worrying about me, and it tugs at my heart in a way it shouldn't. But I haven't figured out how to keep her from affecting me yet. I don't think I ever will.

Does she know how much her presence means to me? Her eyes bore into me, watching with fierce intensity. I wonder what she's thinking, what she's feeling.

Tabby catches her attention, though, throwing her arms around June's waist. June's worry fades when she looks at my daughter, and she smooths Tabby's hair back, smiling down at her. Seeing them together—it's like watching everything in my world align. Having them there for me feels right, like we're an actual family. It's clear June loves my daughter. And I can't help it—I love June.

I'm not an outgoing person. Before Sonya, I barely dated. I met her, and within weeks, I knew she was the one for me. When I lost her, I didn't think I would ever find that kind of connection again. But June makes me feel like sunshine is on my face. Everything is lighter, happier... easier.

I'm not sure what that means in the future. But I'm not the type of person to let the best thing that's happened to me in a long time slip through my fingers.

As the singer finishes, the crowd cheers. I shake my head to clear it. Now isn't the time to think about that. I have a team to lead and a game to win.

The puck drops, and I focus on the game. My mind clears, and I become a machine, moving by muscle memory. We're facing our biggest rivals in game one, and the tension is palpable. The game is fast-paced, and we're neck and neck from the start. But I feel confident, in control. The lines I helped Hargreeves plan are working as well as I could have expected. During the first intermission, we're ahead one to nothing, and I wonder if maybe we have a legitimate chance this year.

In the third period, though, we're tied at two. I have a chance to score. The puck comes to me, and I don't hesitate. I take the shot, and it sails past the goalie's outstretched glove, hitting the back of the net with a satisfying thud. The crowd goes wild, and I feel a rush of pride. This is what I'm good at. This is what I was born to do.

No sooner did the lamp light for my goal, but I take a hard hit from my right. Since I'm still in my follow-through, it catches me in the lower ribs, and I can feel the burn of pain shooting along my side.

I hit the ice, and the crowd boos. Gasping for air, I roll to my side. I need to get up, but my chest is tight. Every breath feels labored. I see the medical team head toward me, but I don't want that, so I wave them off and get to my feet by sheer force of will and skate to the bench.

I can't leave the game. Not now, not when we're so close to winning and not this early in the season. I'm the captain, for fuck's sake. Sure, I'm not young anymore, but I've learned how to power through some discomfort. I nod at my teammates, signaling I'm okay.

My side aches, but I grit my teeth, taking deep breaths, and refuse to acknowledge the pain. I wait for the coach to send me back in. When he finally does, I step onto the ice, feeling the adrenaline surge through me. The pain is still there, but I can bear it.

We're ahead by one goal, and the clock is winding down. I feel the pressure of the game mount on my shoulders. Everyone is counting on me to lead us to victory. I scan the ice, searching for an opening. Then it happens. The net on the other end of the ice is empty, the other team having pulled its goalie for an extra attacker in an attempt to tie the score. The puck comes toward me, and I hit it hard, sending it soaring toward the opposing team's net. Time seems to slow down as I watch it glide through the air, my breath held in anticipation. It hits the back of the net, and the crowd erupts into cheers.

There are only twenty seconds left. We're up by two, and the other team's hopes of winning evaporate. The seconds wind down, and at the final buzzer, we've won.

I skate over to my teammates, my chest heaving with exertion but also with pride. We huddle together, congratulating each other. I exchange a few high fives and pat a couple of backs.

We form a line in front of our goalie, congratulate Huck on a game well played with fist bumps and hugs, skate to center ice to raise our hockey sticks to salute the fans, and then head through the tunnel into the locker room. On my way through, I catch June's eye again.

She beams with happiness as Tabby cheers. My chest tightens, and it has nothing to do with the hit I took earlier.

It's because of my girls.

June

When we get home from the game, I let Tabby have a bowl of ice cream. She won't want to go to bed until Duke gets home, anyway, and he's probably still a half an hour behind us, so we have time.

It's her favorite treat, but I need something sweet and comforting myself, so I fill a bowl of cookie dough, too. I've never watched a full hockey game in person before. When I took this job, I looked up highlights from last year's Tyrants season. But seeing it on a small screen, when the people are tiny and far away, doesn't have the same effect as watching it live.

The game moves so much quicker than I expected. Duke and his teammates skate so fast, I almost couldn't see their puck passes. And the checking? I guess it makes sense the hits are hard if they're moving at high velocity, but I didn't expect the brutality of it. When I saw it on television, I had a panoramic view. Nothing prepared me for how it would feel to watch Duke go down on the ice, right in front of me.

The hit he took stole my breath, like I'd been the one who absorbed the shock of it. When he lay on the ice, stunned, I wanted to throw up. Then there was the anger. How dare that guy hurt Duke? I yelled for a penalty—it had to be a late hit; I was sure—but there was nothing. As Duke stumbled to his feet and skated to the bench, I wanted to hit someone, too.

I couldn't figure out how to process it all, and I still haven't come up with anything by the time Duke walks in the door. Tabby, who has already finished her ice cream, runs to Duke and clings to him. He lifts her up and kisses her forehead. As he leans over to put her down, though, I notice his wince.

"Great game, Daddy," she tells him. "We had ice cream to celebrate."

"Are you sure you didn't just want ice cream?" he teases her.

"June did." Tabby points to me. "It was her idea."

I laugh. "Tattletale."

He shrugs out of his light jacket, favoring his side.

"How are you doing?" I ask, hoping he doesn't notice the quiver in my voice.

I mustn't have hidden my anxiety well because Duke's face grows serious. "Little sore," he says, his hand going to his ribs.

"It looked bad." I'm trying not to sound too concerned. He's not mine to worry about.

He nods. "Yeah, but it'll be fine. It's just a bruise."

I nod, but I can't shake the images of him on that ice. To distract myself, I focus on Tabby. "Come on, Tab. Let's get you showered and into bed."

She fusses, saying it's the weekend, that we should stay up later because it's the team's first win. But I see the dark smudges under her eyes, so I coax her along.

Despite her fight downstairs, she's quiet through showering and brushing her teeth. The excitement must have gotten her because she's sluggish as she creeps under her covers. After hugging her, I make sure she's tucked in to her specifications. I'm not sure why she's got tuck-in requirements since she ends up sprawled out of her covers every night, anyway, but it's just one of the delightful quirks I love about this sweet girl. "I'll send your daddy up to hug you, okay?"

She nods, but her eyelids are already drooping as I head out the door.

I pop my head into the living room and tell Duke she's ready for bed, and then I put away our ice cream dishes. He returns via the kitchen stairs, stretching through his side. My worry flares again.

"Do you need ibuprofen? Something stronger?" I ask. I don't know if there is anything stronger in the house, but I saw we had whiskey behind the bar in the basement. That would probably do the trick.

He shakes his head. "I'm good. Really."

I reach for my phone. "I read something recently, about a salve that's holistic and good for achy muscles. Let me see if I can find it." I flip through the saved websites on my phone until his fingers cover mine. The slight contact is enough to stop me entirely.

"June, you don't have to do all that for me," he murmurs, his hand warm on mine. "I appreciate the concern, but I'll be all right. The team has a trainer. You don't have to go searching for home remedies for me."

I look up at him, and our eyes meet. The air crackles between us with this connection that's been there since I met him. I smell his cologne, and the scent has a calming effect on me. It must be his soap, that fresh evergreen scent. It's hard to hear over the pounding of my pulse in my ears, flooding me with energy. I should step back, move away, but I don't want to. I've never wanted to. He's always had a pull on me, and it's only gotten stronger, no matter how much I've tried to pretend otherwise.

I darken the screen of my phone and put it down, my hand slipping from his grasp. Immediately, I miss the contact. "If you say so. But if you change your mind, let me know."

He nods. "Thank you, June. For coming to my game. I know you wanted to take Tabby, but I wanted to tell you how much it meant to have you there tonight." He swallows, and his eyes are uncertain. "Both of you."

"You're welcome," I breathe out. "I wanted to go." It's the truth. I want to be there for him more than I should. I tell myself it's because he's Tabby's father, but that's a lie. It's because I care about him, and I'm not foolish enough to pretend differently to myself. Not anymore.

I expect him to step back, to put space between us. Over the past couple of weeks, that's what he would do. He hasn't spent much time in my company without Tabby, and I know that's on purpose. It should be easier to not have the temptation of him. But it isn't.

We stand there for a moment, the air between us heavy. I'm not sure what to do. Should I move first? But then he reaches out and tugs a lock of my hair. My breath gets shallow, and I watch him run the strands between his thumb and forefinger. His gaze remains intent on what he's doing, but I can't tear mine from his face.

He's grown some stubble on his cheeks, and it gives him a gruff, almost mysterious vibe. His light eyes are darker than I've ever seen before. Duke keeps a firm grip on his emotions, but he's far from emotionless. If anything, I think he hides his feelings because he feels so intensely. Maybe it scares him, or maybe he's afraid it will scare others. But the way he loves Tabby... it's fierce, protective, and unwavering.

For someone who's never felt like she belonged anywhere, seeing that devotion is intoxicating.

He takes his time, gently stroking my hair as if it's the most precious thing in the world. I'm mesmerized by him, and I don't want to break away.

When our eyes meet, his face is full of conflict. "June," he whispers, leaning forward until our lips are barely an inch apart. His breath brushes against my cheek, and I shiver in anticipation. "Tell me to step away from you." His palms cup my cheek, and his thumbs rub my cheekbones. "Please tell me to stop now because I'm dying to kiss you. I said I wouldn't, but..."

Leaning forward, I close the last space between us. As our lips meet, I close my eyes. He tastes of peppermint and something else, something unique that's just Duke—something that I can't get enough of. His kiss deepens, becoming more desperate as our tongues entwine. I grip him at his waist, drawing him closer, swimming in his taste and scent, relishing the feel of him against me. I never want to let go.

When he pulls away, our breath comes in ragged pants. There's a raw need on his face and in the tension in his body. As our foreheads rest against each other, he holds my face like it's precious while he stares into my eyes.

"I know it's not the right time or the right circumstances, but..." He swallows, and I hate seeing him struggle with words, so I cover his hands with mine. When he continues, it's in a whisper, but his sincerity rings clear. "But I can't stop thinking about you. I've tried to ignore it, but I can't. June, I know it's complicated, but I want to be with you."

The words sing through me. "I feel the same way. I've been trying to deny it, but I can't."

Relief floods his face, and he drops his mouth to mine again. "Stay with me. Tonight. Please."

I smile. "Yes."

He takes my hand and kisses my knuckles, then turns and heads upstairs. As I follow him, I should have reservations. This will change everything. There's no way I'll be able to work for him—take his money—after we sleep together, but I don't care about that right now. Maybe I should. But Duke and Tabby, they're not only a job for me anymore. They're so much more.

Like the rest of my life, I'll figure it out as I go.

Duke

As I lead June up the stairs, holding her hand, I try to remember the reasons this is wrong. I remind myself she is my employee, that my daughter loves her and jeopardizing their relationship is selfish. But I want this woman to stay in our lives forever. She makes everything better, lighter, and happier. So even though I should focus on what's proper, all I can think about is how much I love her.

At the top of the stairs, I pause. "Are you sure you want to do this?" I ask, my voice softening. "A lot can happen from the kitchen to the top of the stairs."

June looks up at me with a teasing grin. "I'm sure."

I squeeze her hand. "We could wait. Think about it some more."

"All I've done for weeks is think about this."

That has parts of my body tightening up that I'm trying to ignore. "Me too, but—"

"Are you trying to talk me out of this?" Her grin slips, and she nibbles her lower lip. "Are you having second thoughts?"

"God no." I sweep forward, covering her mouth again, pulling her against me. She has to feel what she does to me, standing this close. "I want you more than anything. I just don't want to ruin anything else in the process or rush things when we don't need to." I've made my choice. For me, there's no reason to wait. But not everyone is as decisive as I am.

June tilts her head up and wraps her arms around my neck. "Are you worrying about Tabby?"

My fingers tangle in her hair. "Maybe a little. She adores you, and if something goes wrong between us…" I can't even think about that. Nothing will change for me, but I don't know how June feels, what she's thinking. I'm all in, but I can't say the same for her. Am I taking a chance Tabby will get hurt?

June's hands slide down to my chest. "I understand your concerns, but we won't let anything happen to Tabby." The way she says that feels strange, but I know she means it. She would never hurt Tabby on purpose, either.

When she kisses me again, I can't think about it. I'm done trying to resist this woman, and I don't want to keep my hands off her anymore. So, I scoop her up in my arms, and she smothers a laugh, probably to keep from waking Tabby. Hurrying down the hall, I carry her into my bedroom and set her on her feet, closing the door and locking it behind me.

"Tab sleeps like the dead. You know that, right?"

"Can't be too safe."

I wrap my arms around her neck, pulling her closer for another kiss. This time, there's no hesitation, no doubts, just pure desire. I explore her mouth with my tongue, savoring the taste of her, and she moans, her hips arching up to meet mine.

My body reacts to hers in a way that I can't deny. I want her more than anything. Wrapping my arms around her waist, I lift her up, and she wraps her legs around me, her hands digging into my shoulder blades. My lips travel down her neck, kissing and nibbling at her skin, and she lets out a soft moan, her fingers tangling in my hair.

I carry her to the bed and gently set her down. My bed is one of my favorite things in the house. It's an Alaskan king-sized bed, the biggest bed I could buy. Like Tabby, I like to spread out. But I plan to use every inch tonight for June.

She stares up at me, still wearing my hockey jersey and jeans. Her lips are pink from my kisses, and her skin is flushed. I trail a finger along the bridge of her nose, stepping between her legs. "Have I ever told you how much I love your freckles?"

She wrinkles her nose. "You might be the only one, then. Most of the time, I just worry about keeping them covered in sunscreen so they don't multiply." She crosses her eyes at me, and the response is so typically her, I can't help but chuckle.

"Well," I say, "I'm interested in finding out if you have them everywhere."

That wipes the smile off her face, and heat returns to her eyes. Reaching for the hem of her jersey, I lift it over her head along with the long-sleeve sweater she wore under it. She's left in her jeans and the prettiest white lace bra I've ever seen. I go immediately hard. Anyone who has ever said white lingerie is boring hasn't seen June in it.

Her rosy nipples peak in the cool air, visible through the sheer lace. I groan, my body aching for her. Gently, I cup her breasts in my hands, feeling their weight. Her bra clasps in the front, so I make quick work of that, letting the two parts slide down over her shoulders. I lean down to show each nipple equal attention, licking and nibbling at them until June is arching into me. "There are freckles here," I whisper against her skin.

I coax her to lie back, and I hook my thumbs into the waistband of her jeans, dragging them down her long legs until she's lying before me wearing only white lace panties. I take the moment to peruse all of her, from the strands of red hair falling around her face to the tips of her nude toenails. "By the time I'm finished, I want to have licked every one of these freckles. Are you good with that?"

She nods. Her shaky inhale and the blush creeping along her collarbone are irresistible. With quick fingers, I unbutton the dress shirt I wore home and throw it on the floor. Her eyes widen, and I would enjoy her approval more if I wasn't so desperate to taste her. She scoots back as I lower between her legs.

I kneel between her knees, pulling her toward me so her legs hang over the bottom of the bed. Leaning down, I kiss the tops of her thighs, making my way up to the triangle of lace at the center of her. My heart is pounding as I tease her, kissing my way around her panties, but I'm not ready to give us what we want just yet.

This first time I make love to her, I want it to last. I want to make her feel my love because even though I can't tell her the words yet—I know she isn't ready—I can definitely show her.

As a man of my word, I do as I told her I would and kiss as much of her as I can touch. When my lips graze the edge of her panties, and she arches under me, her fingers tangling in my hair. I kiss her hip bone, her ribs, and her stomach. Finally, I slide two fingers under the elastic of her panties and tug them down her legs, discarding them over the side of the bed.

Her hands are restless on my shoulders. "Duke—"

I pause. "You still okay?" I ask. Because if she isn't, this is as far as we go right now.

She watches me, her gaze hot. "Yes," she sighs. "But please. More."

I hush her as I lean over. My eyes hold hers as I graze the backs of my fingers along her inner thigh, moving closer to where she wants me most. I trace the outside of her lips with a single finger, and her mouth falls open on a gasp. Positioned between her thighs, she's open to me. "You're wonderful."

Her fingers dig into the comforter as my tongue finds her. She moans, and as I look up at her, across the planes of her body, she's the picture of lust. Her hair is a riot around her, and her skin is the most delicious shade of pink. I can't get enough. I lick and suck as she moves under me.

My name tumbles out of her mouth as she comes apart under my lips. I keep up the pace until she quiets, and then I gather her against me, holding her close. As she pants, the scent of her body, the feel of her skin, the lingering taste of her in my mouth... I'm as hard as stone, but I've never felt more perfect in my entire life.

I've been alone for a long time, and no one has pierced that darkness. But the woman in my arms fits against me like a wave on the beach, and if she'll have me, I never plan to leave her side.

June

That was a life-changing orgasm. As my heart slows, and I come down, my limbs are blissfully heavy. I curl my body against Duke's. The first thought to pierce the haze is that he's still rock hard behind me. I can feel the length of him pressed into the base of my spine.

I wiggle, turning in his arms, and he groans. "Have some mercy, Freckles."

Glancing up at him, I lift my brows. "Like you had mercy with me?"

He chuckles. "Totally different circumstances."

I shake my head, pressing my palms against his shoulders. He gives in, falling to my back. But his eyes widen when I straddle his upper thighs, resting my hands on his taut stomach. The muscles under my fingers flex, and the sight of him stretched out beneath me makes me hot again. I just came. It seems impossible that I'm already excited again, but that's what he does to me.

"Protection." He points to the nightstand. I lean over. Nothing is in the drawer except a fresh box of condoms.

I tear it open, pulling out an aluminum square. I point to him. "Mind if I sit here?"

He laughs, as I intended, and then his eyes darken. "Absolutely not."

I make quick work of our safety precautions, and then I straddle him. I don't know what he was expecting, but I doubt it was for me to take him inside me immediately.

At first entry, though, he's more than I expect. As I slowly lower myself on him, his eyes are huge, and his fingers dig into my hips. The bite of them only heightens my already sharp desire. I hold his gaze as I seat myself. No part of Duke is small, but I didn't expect to feel this full. No, not full. That part I expected.

Complete. That's the part I didn't bank on.

I press my hands into his chest and stay still for a moment, only watching him. But the look on his face—reverent, hot, and something tender I can't name—forces me to lean forward to kiss him. The change in position makes me cry out, though, and I gasp against his mouth.

"You feel…" I try to come up with an adjective that works, but my mind blanks.

"Fucking amazing," he breathes against my lips. I nod slowly and take his mouth. Our kiss is explosive, and I let it go on and on, with his hands playing across my back. When I break away, he rolls his hips under me. "June… Please…"

Having him below me, begging for me to ride him, makes my anticipation higher. But I'm not ready. He got to kiss and touch. Now it's my turn.

I slowly bend forward, remaining seated hard on him, and run my lips and then my tongue along his chest. He arches up, groaning, as I continue licking and kissing, running my fingers along his skin. I'm careful of his side, where he took his hit today, and even in the dim light I can see the beginning of a bruise on his skin. But all the hours he spends in the gym are on display, and I revel in his strength, in the feel of him. As I continue, he babbles. "Baby, please. I'm... dying. I need..." He sounds breathless, and his hands roam, cupping my breasts, smoothing across my stomach. "If you don't move, I... Please, just fuck... Please, please move."

A surge of power races through me. This gorgeous, protective, generous man is below me, begging me, wanting me. It's heady stuff, and it pushes me to my limit.

I lean back quickly, unable to stay still on him any longer. The change in position steals my breath, and I moan as a bright flare of pleasure streaks through me. The feel of him inside me, the friction... I'm already at the edge of sanity, and I've barely moved yet.

When I lift and lower on him, we both cry out. I adjust my knees so I can move more freely. I planned to go slow, to make this last for us. But as I move, I can't think, can't control my tempo. All I can do is feel and move.

I close my eyes and focus on the rub of him inside me, the heat. His hands cover my breasts, and his thumbs scrape across my nipples, and I say his name, arching against the sensations. When I pick up the pace, the frantic need spiraling inside me, I feel the brush of his fingers against my clit, and I break apart in a crash of feeling and heat.

I gasp, and his hands hold my hips as he moves under me. He follows me over the edge with a groan, and I slow my pace as we come down. Finally, I collapse on top of him, a happy, sweaty heap.

He shifts, pulling out of me, and slides out of the bed. He covers me with the comforter before he heads into the bathroom. Discarding the condom, I guess. But he's back quickly, and he pulls me into his arms. Tucking my head on his chest, he cocoons me with his warmth and covers us both up.

"Did you want me to go to my room?" I ask.

"Never," he says immediately. Then he amends, "In a little while you can go. If you want." Then he cups the back of my head, and his entire body softens. I swear, it's not even a minute before his breath is even and slow.

My body is lazy, and I want to follow him into sleep, but my mind is buzzing.

Sex with Duke is magical. I could always feel the connection between us, but tonight was beyond anything I could have imagined. I meant it when I told him we wouldn't let anything hurt Tabby. I don't quite understand what is going to happen now. I'll need to find a new job, some way to make money. No way I'm cashing this week's paycheck.

My mind wants to drag me down into all the possible troubles, but right now, in Duke's arms, I'm too pleasure drunk to do anything but dose off.

Duke

THE TEAM HOLDS THE Tyrants Charity Carnival that Sunday afternoon. The charity group that runs the carnival raises money for nonprofit organizations in the greater Philadelphia area. Literacy, food insecurity, homelessness, addiction... the money we raise does a lot of good helping to address the problems in the community. It's a huge event, and the entire team brings their families to support it.

I take Tabby and June. Tabby has always loved this event, and watching my daughter's joy makes it worth fighting the crowds. June? I bring her because I want to spend time with her.

Yesterday, I had another game at home, but June and Tabby didn't go to this one. It was about dinnertime when I got home, and we had a movie night. This time we watched the first Harry Potter movie and had tacos. After we put Tabby to bed, we curled on the couch and watched a Marvel movie together and then made love into the night. Between lovemaking, we talked about everything. I told her about Sonya, and she asked a million questions about her, about what raising Tabby alone had been like.

I asked June about her mother, but she didn't say much, only that she'd been an addict who couldn't care for her. She was much more willing to talk about Lily, who she clearly adores. We talked about her degrees.

It was a picture-perfect night. But tomorrow starts our first stretch of road games. I won't be home until Thursday, so I plan to make the most of this last day with June and Tabby before I leave.

They set rides up in the parking lot, including a Ferris wheel and a carousel. Some guys have volunteered for the dunk tank and to work at a handful of game stations. There's fried food everywhere—funnel cakes, fried Oreos, and French fries.

As we weave through the crowd, the sound of laughter and screaming children fills the air. Walking next to June and holding Tabby's hand fills me with contentment I haven't felt in a very long time. Frequently, people ask me for my autograph, and I oblige. We pass by the cotton candy stand, and I promise Tabby we'll get some on our way out. I agree to try our luck at some of the game stations.

Tabby wins a stuffed animal at the ring toss, and June gets a ball in the clown's mouth at the beanbag toss.

Huck is working the baseball throw and calls out to me. "Duke York, our fearless captain. I think you should come and win a prize for your lovely ladies." Everyone in the immediate area turns at his booming voice. Fucking Huck. He knows I hate being the center of attention.

I glare at him, holding up my hands. "That's okay. I'll save the prizes for our fans."

There's a collective groan of disappointment, and Huck encourages it. Bastard. "What do you think, everyone? Don't you think Duke should try his hand at our game?"

I roll my eyes but can't keep the smile off my face. Huck always brings some fun to the charity carnival.

Tabby tugs on my sleeve. "Come on, Dad! Let's play!"

I feel the eyes of the crowd on me, and I can sense their eagerness for me to accept Huck's challenge. I've never been great at baseball, and I definitely hate being put on the spot. But I know I can't back down now. This is for charity. So, I pay my entry fee, take a deep breath, and step up to the plate.

Huck hands me a baseball, grinning like a fool. "Show us what you got, Duke!"

I glare at him as I grip the ball, taking a moment to aim. I let it fly and watch as it sails through the air, hitting the target with a satisfying thud. A small cheer erupts from the crowd, and I can't help but feel a sense of pride.

Huck hands me another ball, and I repeat the process. This time, I miss the target, and the crowd groans in disappointment. Huck jumps into the strife, playing up the drama. "Look out, folks. Duke is about to leave his girls with no prizes."

I want to give him the finger, but this is a family function. I settle for, "Shut up, Huck."

Inhaling, I clear my mind. I've never been one to back down, and I haven't gotten where I am in my career by letting pressure get to me. There's no way I'm not winning something now. I focus on the target, picturing the ball hitting dead center. I let it go, and it soars through the air, hitting the target with a loud smack.

The crowd erupts into cheers and applause.

Huck hands me a small stuffed animal. "Way to go, old man."

"Fuck off," I whisper to him. "I'm younger than you."

He laughs. Smiling, I wave to the crowd and hand the prize to Tabby, who is beaming with pride. "Thanks, Dad!" she says, hugging the stuffed animal close.

"What about your girlfriend?" someone calls out, and in a split second, others join in.

I feel June stiffen next to me. But when I face her, she's hidden her emotions behind a smile. She shakes her head, waving off the crowd. "Thanks everyone, but I'm good," she says, laughing it off.

But the group gathered around isn't having it. "Should I play again?" I ask, even though I didn't even want to play the first time.

"Kiss her!" someone calls out.

In front of me, June turns bright red. I can see Huck over her shoulder, his eyebrows high. I have no idea what to do in this situation. Beside me, Tabby has her hands folded, the same starry-eyed look on her face that she gets when we watch princess movies. Except this is a potential disaster.

Kiss her, and everyone will know how I feel, including June. Something like that would scream commitment, and what if she's not ready for that? Now isn't the time I want to find that out.

I lean forward and brush my lips across June's cheekbone. When I retreat, her gaze is intense on my face. Her lips part slightly, and I can see her pupils have flared, but I hope no one else notices. With as much nonchalance as I can manage, I shift away from her and wave. Then I snag Tabby's hand and cup June's elbow, leading them both away from Huck's stand.

As we walk away, I can sense June's eyes still on me, and I'm sure she's curious about what just happened. I'm torn between worrying I went too far and being irritated I couldn't go further. But I can't rush things with her. Too much is at stake with Tabby in the mix.

Tabby chatters away as we make our way through the various attractions at the fair. We stop at the carousel, and I buy Tabby a ticket. She insists she doesn't need help to get up on her horse, so June and I watch from the makeshift fence around the ride.

As it turns, the animals bobbing up and down, I say, "I'm sorry if that made you awkward back there."

June's expression softens. "It's okay," she says. "I just wasn't expecting it." She pauses, her gaze flickering down to her hands. "But I didn't hate it."

I grin, my shoulder bumping hers. "You didn't?"

June shakes her head, a smile quirking at the corner of her lips and her dimple on display. "Not at all."

I lean closer. "Do you want me to do it again?"

"Yes," she says without hesitation. "But not here." Her eyes drift to where Tabby is waiting for us to wave at her on this pass.

I nod, forcing down the conflicting emotions again. When Tabby is done, we make our way inside the rink. I'm scheduled to do some pictures, and I suggest June and Tabby go and public skate until I'm done.

June's eyes flare. "Oh, I don't know how to skate." She lifts her hands, shaking her head.

Tabby grabs her hand. "Come on, June. You can do it."

"Tab, you've seen me dance. Do you think skating's a good idea?" Genuine anxiety is on her face. "I barely balance when I'm on dry land. I'm pretty sure I'm not going to be very good on skates."

Tabby gives her a reassuring smile. "It's okay, June. You can only get good at something by being bad at it first."

Those are words I've said to Tabby more than once, but I can tell by June's expression she's not buying it. The trepidation on her face is a punch to my stomach. No way is my girl feeling like that when I can help it. Heading over to the photo both, I ask if I can take the shift after this one instead, and Rocco Barnett is there, so he agrees to take my spot.

"Come on," I say, taking June's hand. "I'll help you."

"Oh, Duke," she sighs out. "You have no idea what you're getting into."

"Oh, June, I think I do," I reassure her, chuckling. "I have seen you dance. And play basketball. I have my suspicions about how this will go."

"And you still want to skate with me?" She looks skeptical, but it's more than that. It's something vulnerable.

"Yes." I don't understand what's going through her head right now, but I don't like it.

Tabby pipes in. "We'll both help you. Dad's a great skater, and I'm not too bad either." I want to laugh at the understatement of the seven-year-old. I'm a professional hockey player. Skating is my job. But June looks pained, like she's bracing herself. My laughter dies in my throat.

June and Tabby rent skates, and I run into the locker room for mine before I help them lace up. When we get to the edge of the ice, Tabby takes June's hand. "Just take it slow, June. Keep your feet pointed straight ahead and don't lean too far to either side. You'll get the hang of it."

I feel a burst of pride, watching my daughter encourage someone she cares about. But I suspect it'll be harder for June than just trying not to lean too far.

I hop onto the ice, feeling that familiar zing. There's nowhere in the world better than a sheet of ice. I skate backward and hold my hands out to June. "Here," I tell her. "Lean on me."

June looks at me like I'm crazy. "Don't you need to see where you're going?"

I roll my eyes, then I take off, zigzagging and weaving around in the crowd while skating backward. When I return to her, she scowls at me. "You could have just told me you'd be fine skating backward, you show-off."

I laugh, reaching for her hands and giving them a squeeze. "Tabby, you good?"

My daughter nods, jumping the marble threshold to the ice, and taking off. Tabby's been on skates since she could walk, the same as me.

June? I think she's going to be a bit more complicated.

"You ready to give this a try?" I ask.

She inhales a steadying breath. "Let's do it, hockey man."

June

As soon as my blades hit the ice, I know I'm going to suck at ice skating. Still, I've never been one to shy away from trying something new. I step forward, gripping Duke's forearms. Offhand, I notice again what fantastic arms and shoulders he has. Like everything else on him, they're muscular, perfectly shaped. But I can't think about that too long because I'm too busy trying to stay upright.

Duke chuckles at my wobbling, but he doesn't let go of my arms. He doesn't seem to mind how hard I lean on him, either. "You've never skated before?" he asks.

"Shush," I tell him, focusing on the ice in front of my feet. "No talking. I need to concentrate."

"Just relax."

"If I relax, I'll fall." We haven't even gone halfway around the rink, and my feet already hurt.

He lifts a shoulder. "I fall all the time."

I jerk my gaze up to his, which moves my head, almost throwing me off-balance. My fingers tighten on him. "No, you don't."

"Well, not as much anymore. But I used to."

"Yeah, but you're naturally athletic." I've never seen him do one clumsy thing. He moves like a man who's completely comfortable in his body. Even the fall he took at the game the other night was graceful. "I'm definitely not."

"Well, you're naturally wonderful," he fires back, and I'm so surprised by the comment, I lose my balance.

I stumble forward, and Duke catches me before I hit the ice. I can feel his muscular arms around me, pulling me up against his chest. The heat radiating off his body is intoxicating, and for a moment, I forget how to breathe. My heart rate spikes as I look up at him, our faces only inches apart. His breath is warm against my face.

My brain floods with images of last night. Not just the sex, though that was the best of my life. But I can't stop thinking of holding him, of waking up in the dark next to his warm, sleep-softened body. It felt so good. I wanted to stay, and that's why I crept into the quiet hallway and back to my room, the same as I did the first time we made love. I need to be very careful with those urges. We slept together, and it was amazing. That doesn't mean this is a serious thing. I care about Duke, and Tabby has my heart. It's important I proceed with caution. I haven't even told him I can't take his money any longer. There are so many details we need to work out.

"You okay?" he asks, one hand resting on the small of my back.

I look up at him, getting lost in his light eyes. "Yeah," I whisper, feeling a flush creep up my neck. His muscles tense beneath my fingers as he steadies me. For a moment, we stand there, looking at each other. Then, slowly, he steps back.

"Thanks," I say, my voice a little breathless.

He smiles down at me, and my heart flutters in my chest. "Anytime," he replies, still grinning at me. "Are you ready to try it without holding on to me?"

"Absolutely not," I answer quickly, and he laughs.

"Sounds good. I like to hold you, anyway."

"Are you flirting with me?" I tease, trying to break the tension. We're in public. We need to be discreet.

"That depends. Do you like it?" He wiggles his eyebrows.

"I do."

"Then yes." He nods solemnly. "I am."

I laugh, which makes me unbalanced again, and I grip his hands. "Duke York, you're almost charming when you want to be."

At that, he performs some sort of twist and dips me into his arms, like we're ballroom dancing. My hair cascades toward the ice. My breath hitches, and I can feel the heat spreading through my body. We're still in public, but I can't seem to care. Not when Duke is holding me like this with that look on his face. I don't understand what's happening between us, but it's heady and addictive. "I'm not charming," he whispers. "You've charmed me."

As he lifts me back up, I can feel my cheeks flush with heat. I can see on his face that he wants to kiss me, and I want him to.

Tabby skids to a stop next to us. "Whatchu guys doing?" she asks, and we step apart so fast, I'm surprised I don't wipe out again.

"Nothing, baby," Duke says. "Just helping June out."

"He's going to help me get off the ice. My legs are killing me." It's the truth, but I also need a break from being so close to him, or I'm going to end up in some PDA.

With his help, I make it to the edge of the rink, albeit slowly and awkwardly. He helps me sit down on a bench. I'm breathing heavily, and my legs feel like jelly.

"Thanks for helping me out and being patient with me," I say, grinning up at him.

"Please. It was fun. No extra patience needed." He kneels in front of me, unlacing my skates.

"It was fun making sure I didn't break my face skating?" I roll my eyes. "You must be joking."

His hands pause on my skates, and he glances up at me, his expression serious. "Spending time with you, doing anything, is more fun than I've had in longer than I can remember."

The words steal my breath and anything I might have considered saying next. "Duke..." I don't know what comes next. He mustn't, either, because he shifts to sit next to me.

"You should be able to slide those off now," he says, motioning to the skates. "I'm going to go do a few laps with Tabby. Are you okay here for a few minutes?"

I scan his face, looking for some sign of what he's thinking. But I'm confused, tired, and flustered, and I can't read his expression and don't understand what's going on here. So, I nod, and he squeezes my arm before he hops up and heads back out to the ice.

I put my sneakers back on and watch Duke and his daughter mess around together. He sweeps her up into his arms, and she laughs, and my chest aches. They're so much alike. Both quiet and reserved, but underneath, they're sensitive and feel things intensely. It's impossible not to want to be important to them, and my heart melts.

I'm afraid this won't end well for any of us.

Monday morning, Duke leaves with the team for two away games. After he's gone, I visit a blood testing center, and they take vial after vial of blood. There are a few tests to determine if a patient and a potential donor are a kidney match. These samples will determine, through blood typing, tissue typing, and crossmatching, if Lily will accept my kidney or not.

It's not my right, but I miss sleeping next to Duke on Monday night.

Tuesday, I distract myself by calling Violet and meeting her for lunch. She's working as a financial analyst in Philadelphia, so I take the train in. I suggest we stop at the food court at the mall, but she insists on treating me at a posh bistro around the corner from her work. It's feeling like fall, so we sit outside on the restaurant patio. Violet has a glass of wine with her salad, but I refrain. I tell her to congratulate Hunter on making the team, and she asks a ton of subtle but pointed questions about my relationship with Duke. It's fun to catch up with her.

On Wednesday, I'm sitting with Lily for her morning dialysis. She's bloated, and seeing the signs of her kidneys failing reminds me we're running out of time. The lab assured me it wouldn't take long to get the results, but I'm still anxious. Lily waves me off, but I can tell she's only trying to make me feel better. After I return her to her assisted living facility, I drive home with fifteen minutes to spare until Tabby gets off the bus.

When I turn off the engine, my phone comes out of driving mode and signals I have a voicemail. It's Tabby's teacher, Miss Shepherd, so I dial her back as I head inside.

"Thank you for calling me back so quickly," she says after our greetings.

"Absolutely." I've emailed back and forth with Miss Shepherd as we make our way through Tabby's testing approval. "I know how important it is to be available."

"And teachers appreciate that more than you know." Miss Shepherd chuckles. "I was going to email, but it's just as easy to call. I'll email you the list of tests we've scheduled for Tabby. Most of them will be in the building here, but a couple will need to be conducted at the district office. After we have those results, we can schedule a full meeting with everyone to go over everything and come up with a final plan of action. I hope that both you and Mr. York will attend."

"When you know, I'll clear it with Mr. York. We'll definitely be there."

"Wonderful. I'll send you the paperwork as we get it."

"Thank you, Miss Shepherd."

"Absolutely." She pauses, then says, "I don't know if it's my place, but I wanted to let you know there's a long-term substitute teaching position that will be available after Thanksgiving. It's one of the special education teachers in the second-grade pod. I recall you said you just graduated from Rutgers and you're dually certified, correct? General and special education?"

"I am." My heart rate picks up.

"Well, I wanted to bring the position to your attention." She exhales slowly. "We could use someone like you in our department."

I don't know what to say. I've only met Miss Shepherd once. "How do you know?" I ask before I can stop myself.

She laughs softly. "I've been teaching for ten years. I know a lot about people. You have good intentions. Honestly, that's the most important part of teaching, I think."

I thank her for considering me and hang up. I'm standing on the porch, about to go in and drop my purse, but I sit down on one of the rocking chairs there instead.

It's a late October day, and the weather is perfect for a fair-skinned girl like me. Mid-sixties, so I'm in jeans and a sweater. Tucking one leg under myself, I push the rocking chair with the other, allowing the rhythm to soothe me.

This teaching job might be the piece of the puzzle to assuage my worries. If it doesn't start until after the holidays, that would give me time to help Lily first. I assume the transplant would make dialysis unnecessary, so she won't need me as much after long. A substitute position wouldn't require the same amount of work as if I got hired in a full-time position, I assume. But I could still be there for Tabby, if Duke would still want me to live here. We haven't talked about that aspect of our relationship. Everything is new to us. I don't think either of us wants to rock the boat.

I haven't told him I won't accept my paycheck on Friday. I keep meaning to, but I feel like it'll upset him, so I haven't. But I need to. When he gets back from his trip, I'll broach the subject. Maybe by then I'll know more about whether I'm a match for Lily.

Surely there is a way to work all of this out, for me to take care of all the people I care about. I just feel like I'm destined to let one of them down.

Duke

WEDNESDAY NIGHT, I CALL June after my game in Chicago. It's late by the time I get to the hotel—almost eleven—so it's nearly midnight in New Jersey. But she picks up my call.

"Hello?" Her voice is raspy, like she's tired, but it heats me up and soothes me at the same time.

"Hey, Freckles. You're still up."

"You called me," she points out. "Why would you call me if you didn't think I'd be up?"

"I hoped you'd be up. That's different from assuming you're still up."

"Semantics, York."

I chuckle. It's so good to talk to her.

"I saw the game," she says.

"You did? How did I do?" I ask as I stretch out on the bed. I'm irrationally pleased she watched. She's said before she doesn't know much about hockey.

"Please. You know you're amazing, Duke."

I warm at the compliment. "How are you? How's Tabby?"

"We're good. Tabby's snoring."

"Of course."

"I talked with her teacher. They're scheduling a bunch of tests. Once all of the results are available, we'll meet with the child study team to discuss our next steps. It should be a few weeks, they think."

"Okay. Just add it to our calendar when you have the details, and I'll make it." At the start of the season, we set up an electronic calendar we could put shared appointments on. June thought it would be easier to manage, considering all my traveling.

"Great. I'll email Miss Shepherd and let her know."

Talk of appointments reminds me of something I've been meaning to tell her. "Sonya's mom is back in town. She finished her rehab in Switzerland. Her name is Nancy. I was hoping I could introduce her to you. She's really a great person, and she loves Tabby very much."

"I'd love to meet her," June says automatically, as I knew she would. She's never met a person she didn't want to know better. "Why don't we have her for dinner tomorrow night when you get back?"

My heart twists. I love this woman so much. "I'd love that," I say. And I love you, I add in my head.

"Great. What can I make?"

"Don't go nuts," I caution, even though I am fully aware she's going to do what she wants. "And Nancy loves everything. She's not picky." She can't be. Sonya's mother is as bad a cook as I am. When you suck at feeding yourself, everything is an improvement.

"Okay, I'll sort it out with Tabby."

"Sounds good." I smile, just happy to hear her voice. "I miss you, June."

I'm not sure if I mean to say the words, but I don't regret them. They're true, and I've never been one to pretend things aren't the way they are. This trip has been so much harder than other road trips. Usually, I only need to deal with missing Tabby, which is already hard. But adding the ache of missing June too? It's made the days feel long. Plus, I took a hit tonight that left my knee aching. My body is getting too busted for this job.

There's a long silence, and I don't break it. I keep getting closer and closer to telling June how I feel about her, but it seems like every time I mention anything close to serious, to declarations of affection, she shies away. I'm doing my best to be patient. It hasn't even been a week since we slept together for the first time.

"I miss you too," she finally says softly, and the words sing through me. I feel triumphant, like a Roman conqueror, or like I went out and hunted to support her with my own hands. It's a stupid, possessive feeling, but I don't care. "We need to talk about something, though."

If I was ecstatic after her admission that she missed me, the next phrase drops me off that high. "Do we?" I ask, doing my best to keep the trepidation out of my voice. "What's up?"

"I can't take my paycheck anymore."

That's not what I expected her to say. "What?"

"We're sleeping together, Duke," she offers.

"I actually love that we're sleeping together." My mind races. I assumed our relationship would change. In my mind, everything is different. But this wasn't what I was thinking about.

"Me too. But it means I can't take your paychecks now."

Why didn't I see this coming? I know this woman. She's proud, smart. If I'd been thinking straight, I would have predicted this. But I wasn't paying attention, apparently. Why didn't I consider how this would change her financial situation? Because I never think about money. Before I ever had to worry about having enough to pay my bills, I had a multi-million dollar contract with the Tyrants. That was a decade ago, and I hired smart financial advisers. After I retire, I won't have to work again if I don't want to.

June isn't that fortunate. I want to tell her the money is the least of my concerns. But our relationship complicates things.

"June..." I drag her name out, trying to organize my thoughts.

"Duke..." she teases. "It's okay. I knew. When we slept together, I knew."

That makes me feel even more uncomfortable. "You knew you'd be out of income when you slept with me?" That is not a thing I was thinking about that night. That she had been thinking about it shows exactly how different our circumstances were.

"Sure." She says it like it's a natural assumption. "But Tabby's teacher mentioned there's a long-term sub position opening after Thanksgiving. If I take that, I'll be working the same hours as Tabby is in school. It won't interfere with me taking care of her."

Something feels off about the way she says all of this, but I'm struggling to place it. "Do you want to do that? To teach after the holidays?"

"The only reason I didn't teach this year was because I didn't want the stress of a new teaching position with Lily's health the way it is. I'm hopeful Lily's situation stabilizes soon, and I'll be able to do this and still help you."

If June had taken a full-time position this year, Tabby and I wouldn't have met her. The thought leaves me cold. "You don't need to take a different job, June. You can just stay with us."

I know as soon as I say the words that they're wrong. She responds with clipped words. "I'm sorry. I can't do that."

"June—"

"I spent my childhood being a burden or feeling like a freeloader. I refuse to feel like that as an adult." The words drop like a grenade in our conversation.

I knew I fucked up, but this is a different level. I never considered the toll growing up like she did had on her. My own parents are still together in Canada. They were university sweethearts and have been together since. My father owns a large construction company, and my mother is a mortgage officer. My childhood was stable and ordinary, boring even. The opposite of hers. "I'm sorry. I didn't mean it like that."

"I know you didn't." Her tone is softer but not less firm.

"I just—" I inhale. "I didn't think about this when—"

"When you slept with me?" She chuckles. "I know. I mean, I knew things would change. I just wasn't sure how it would work out. But it will. Don't worry."

The way she says it makes me think this won't be the end of these kinds of conversations, and I can't help wondering what other shoes there are to drop.

Would it help if I told her I loved her? That I want her to stay with me, to marry me? I don't know. I doubt it, and it makes me feel helpless in a way I don't like. "I can't wait to see you tomorrow," I finally say.

"Me too. What time will you be home?"

I love the way she says home. "Midafternoon."

"Great. And I'll make sure we have something yummy for Nancy."

After what she just said about not accepting a paycheck, I worry she could feel like I'm taking advantage of her. I hate that feeling.

Why didn't I consider this earlier? "Thank you," I finally say, because what else can I do now? I'm not good at this stuff. I wish I was there. I'm sure I would handle this better in person.

"I can't wait to see you tomorrow," I repeat. There's nothing truer.

"Good night, Duke," she says softly. "Sleep well."

We hang up, but I'm left with an unsettled feeling in my stomach. When I get home, I'll figure out a way to smooth all of this over. Maybe the way we got together wasn't ideal, but it isn't anything that we can't sort out for the future. We just need to work out the kinks.

June

Nancy doesn't like me.

I had been looking forward to meeting Tabby's grandmother. From the way Tabby describes her Nana, she sounds like a caring, fun person. Duke has only spoken about Nancy with respect. But it's clear from the second she arrives at the house that she has no intention of befriending me.

I decide to put chicken noodle soup on the stove, and I make a loaf of bread. Tabby assures me Nana likes soup, so I figure I'm safe. It's a chilly day, too, so I wanted to offer her something warm and comforting. I made an apple pie for dessert.

The second Nancy steps in the door, she scans me from head to toe and dismisses me. It's a subtle thing. A cursory glance, nothing drawn out, but I've been on the receiving end of glances like that before. I recognize it for what it is.

When she sees Tabby, though, she folds her into a tight hug, keeping one hand on the cane she favors. "My girly! I'm so glad to see you."

Tabby hugs her back, a huge grin on her face. "How's your leg, Nana?"

Nancy stands up again, leaning on her cane again. She pats her right leg. "I'm out of a cast now, so they flew me back home. I can drive, and that's the most important part. So, I can come see you. I should be as good as new soon."

Tabby squeezes her again. "I'm so glad. I missed you." She steps away and joins me. "This is June, my nanny."

Nancy looks me up and down once again, her lips pursed. "Hmm," she says, noncommittally. "Nice to meet you, June."

I smile my most likable smile. I'm not sure what I did to offend her, but I can feel her dislike for me rolling off her in waves. "Thank you for coming."

She snorts. "It's my son-in-law and granddaughter's home. Of course, they would be my first stop."

"Absolutely," I agree.

"Nancy," Duke says, coming downstairs. He got home earlier and went up to shower and catch a quick nap before dinner. There are still dark circles under his eyes, though. He's already exhausted, and he leaves again with the team tomorrow for Boston. "I'm so glad to see you moving around." He leans in to kiss her cheek. "I see you've met June."

As always, Duke's eyes are warm when he looks at me, and his presence soothes me. "We did," I offer her another smile. Nancy doesn't return it.

"Your nanny, huh?" She harrumphs again before holding her arm out to Duke. "Hon, will you help me into the living room? I just need to sit down. My leg is still giving me trouble."

"Sure," he says, steadying her. He casts me a questioning glance, and I only shake my head with a small shrug. "Let's get you settled."

"Come keep me company, Tabby?" Nancy asks.

Tabby skips to join them, clearly happy to have her grandmother back. She chatters away as they go into the living room, and I'm left in the foyer alone. Nancy's message is obvious—I don't belong here.

Taking a deep breath, I head into the kitchen to make sure everything's ready for dinner. I put together a salad, so I dress that and warm the bread, setting everything out. When the meal is ready, I call to everyone.

Duke helps Nancy into the dining room, and Tabby sits next to her. She's talking about the library upstairs. "Daddy had all the walls of the playroom covered in shelves, so June and I have somewhere to read." I love hearing her excitement about the books.

Nancy casts a quick glance at Duke. "Did you, now?"

Duke only grunts, his eyes on the food. I want to glare at him, but I can't make eye contact. He's either too clueless to the tension in the room or he's too hungry to care.

I sit across from Nancy, determined to make conversation as if nothing is wrong. "Nancy, they told me you hurt yourself skiing. How long have you been skiing? Do the doctors think you'll be able to ski again?"

She gives me an assessing glare and then falls into conversation. At first, things are fine as we eat our dinner and talk about Nancy's time in the hospital and rehab. She sounds like an incredibly active person, and my guess is she hated being unable to do the things she wanted. I completely understand that. I think I would make a terrible patient, too.

Tabby wolfs down her food and asks to be excused. When Duke nods, she hugs us all and runs into the living room.

With her gone, Nancy turns to me. "Tell me about yourself, June. Where did you grow up?"

I pat my lips with my napkin. "My mother and I lived all over when I was young, and then I was in foster care from middle school until I graduated from high school. My foster mother lives in Moorestown, so that's where I went to school, and then I studied education at Rutgers."

She makes a noncommittal hum. "I see." She turns to Duke, and her voice is full of censure. "So," she begins, "you think it's okay to hire someone else to raise your child?"

I swallow hard, taken aback. Duke clears his throat. If he didn't know there was animosity in the air before, he does now.

He glances between Nancy and me, as if trying to get his bearings. "You know how much I travel, Nan. It's important for Tabby to have someone consistent here. June is her friend and confidante, which I'm sure you can appreciate." He looks at me. "She's become irreplaceable to me as well."

Heat is in his eyes, and his words fill me with happiness, even as Nancy's eyes narrow. "There are certain proprieties that must be observed in a single-parent household. Don't you think it's inappropriate for a young woman to be living here with a single man?" She turns her gaze back on Duke, her expression stern. "You need to remember that."

Duke's face is grim. "Don't hold back on my account, Nan. Christ."

"There's something going on between you." It's an accusation. Although my heart is pounding from the reprimand, I know that Nancy only wants what she believes is best for Tabby. She's her grandmother. It's her right to worry.

What I am, exactly? The hired help? Duke's closet girlfriend?

I inhale and stand. I'm someone who cares about Duke and Tabby, but this isn't a conversation I should be part of. "I'm going to go see if Tabby is okay before I clean up the kitchen. Let me know if either of you needs anything. Please excuse me."

I escape, hurrying into the living room with Tabby.

Duke

"What is wrong with you?" I hiss at Nancy across the dining room table. "You're being nasty." Since Sonya passed, Nancy and I have been close. We were both mourning, and I needed help with Tabby. She became a parent figure to me as well since my family is in Canada. But I've never met this version of her. Since she got here and met June, she's been angry and snappy.

"You're in love with her," she whispers back. She says it like I've done something wrong, and it sets me on the defensive.

"I am." There's no reason to deny it. Gritting my teeth, I try to control my anger. "I'm allowed to be in love, Nan. I've been alone for a long time."

"Have you lost your mind?"

I can only blink at her. "No. I'm trying to be happy. Sonya has been gone for almost eight years, but Tabby and me, we need to keep living."

Nancy's head jerks as if I slapped her, and I feel immediately guilty. I'm not trying to hurt her, but she had to realize I might find someone new someday. Did she expect me to be alone forever? She's known me since I was twenty years old. I'm a serious person. I don't even have a lot of friendships, preferring a few close friends. Huck. My friend Max, who got traded to Seattle a couple of years ago. But I have had no significant relationships since Sonya died. When Tabby was small, I dated a few women, but it didn't feel right, and I'm not one to push things that don't fit.

Nancy has to realize June is special to me. June fits.

She narrows her eyes. "You think that girl is a suitable replacement for Sonya? She's so young. And a foster child?" She shakes her head. "Please tell me what she knows about being a mother to a seven-year-old child. It doesn't sound like she comes from any sort of stability at all. Do you think this is what Sonya would have wanted for her baby?"

"She's not a replacement. There isn't any replacement for Sonya." My words are low and sharp, but they don't hide my outrage. "I'm not trying to replace anyone." How could she say that? If I was just looking for a replacement mother for my daughter, wouldn't I have found one a long time ago?

"This girl—"

"Her name is June, and you don't even know her." I stand. "And we don't know what Sonya would have wanted. Back then, she wanted to be with me, with her daughter. But that's not what happened. I can't change any of that. All I have is right now, and June makes me..." I search for the proper words. "She makes things alive again." Nancy looks away, but I can see the color on her cheeks. I soften my tone. "I'm not trying to hurt you, Nan. But I'm Tabby's father. You need to believe I'm doing what's right by her. And June is right. I hope you'll be happy for us."

She shakes her head and presses a finger to the corner of her eye, swiping away a tear. My heart aches. I can't imagine what she must be going through. Sonya's dad died of a massive heart attack ten years ago, and then Nan lost Sonya a few years later. I've always considered her to be part of my family, and I want that to continue. But I can't live in the past. I hope she'll come to understand that.

"I'm happy you're home," I say, and it's true. Tabby has missed her.

Nancy nods, glancing up at me, the feelings raw in her eyes. "Yes." She swipes at her face, as if irritated by her emotions. "I'd like to see Tabby more again. If you don't mind me taking some nights that you're out of town, maybe? I can sleep here, or Tabby can come to my house, like she used to. Maybe tomorrow night? I've missed her."

"Absolutely, Nancy." I am trying to follow what's going on with her. "June's presence doesn't change how important you are to us."

"Of course, of course," she nods, but the movement is jerky. I round the table and hug my mother-in-law. We've all been through so much together.

"I should go," Nancy says, her voice choked up. She places her palms on the table, using the leverage to help her get up.

"Sounds good," I say. Nancy collects her bag and calls Tabby for a hug. My daughter comes bounding out of the living room and squeezes her grandmother before running back to whatever she was watching. I notice June stays away. I can't say I blame her. After the way Nancy acted, June is probably afraid Nancy will cause another scene.

As Nancy leaves, I can't help but feel a weight lift off my shoulders. I understand she's got reservations, and I won't pretend to understand her grieving process. But I know deep down that I am doing what is best for our family.

I turn around to see June standing in the doorway. "Is everything okay?" she asks, concern etched in her voice.

I nod, walking toward her. "Yeah." I wrap my arms around her waist, pulling her close. Tabby's in the other room, so I steal this moment with June. "I'm sorry. About Nancy."

"It's okay," she says. "She's recovering from her injury, and she's probably worried this means she'll get less time with Tabby." She glances away, though. We both know that's not it. June's just being gracious. But I don't know how to explain what Nancy might be dealing with because I don't understand it either. I can't imagine the pain of losing a child, and I don't even want to try.

Right now, I'm more exhausted than I've been in a long time. "Let me help clean up, and then I'll get Tabby through her shower."

"You go ahead. I've got it." She smiles, but it's guarded, and I hate it. "I'm sure you've missed her." Turning, she heads into the kitchen without another word.

With nothing I can think of to say, I call to Tabby.

June

After I finish cleaning the kitchen, I go up to my room to regroup. While I was in the living room with Tabby, I didn't listen in on the conversation happening in the dining room on purpose, but I couldn't help hearing. They weren't really keeping their voices down, especially toward the end.

Nancy thinks I'm trying to replace her daughter. The idea fills me with ice. I don't want to take anyone's place. My whole life, I've only been trying to find my own place.

Duke seemed to calm her down. He told her he was just trying to be happy. I can't help thinking that every time I think things are going to work out for us, there seems to be something else that complicates things.

To distract myself, I plop down on my bed and check my email. My heart races as I see an email from Dr. Jones. He's the doctor who has been looking into whether I could be a donor for Lily. I click to open the email, and my eyes scan over the words.

Dear Ms. Harlow,

We are pleased to inform you that you're a match as a kidney donor for...

I can't read anymore because tears blur my eyes. After all my worrying about her, it looks like I'll be able to help Lily after all.

Standing, I swipe at my eyes and read the rest of Dr. Jones's email. There's a time frame listed and some preparations that will need to be done. But it seems like the procedure will be completed in the next few weeks, sooner even. I will need to talk with Lily and convince her this is the right step. She just needs to understand all the benefits, and I'll give her all the information. I did some research over the past few days. I can still live a full life with one kidney. The research warned against playing contact sports, but I suck at sports, anyway. Not being able to play them won't change my life at all.

There's a knock on my door. Duke pokes his head in. "Hey. Tabby would like a hug if that's okay? Then maybe you could come see me in my room?" He lifts his eyebrows suggestively.

I grin at him and nod. As I scoot past him at the door, I plant a kiss on his cheek. Right now, I feel like everything is going to be okay. Things with Lily are working out. That's a step in the right direction. I hurry down the hall to hug Tabby.

She's already got sleepy eyes. "Did you like my Nana?"

"She's your grandmother. Of course, I like her." That much is true. Anyone who is special to the little girl is special to me. I lean over and hug her.

"I'm glad. I love you, June," she says, rolling over. "Good night."

My throat tightens. I smooth my hand over her crazy blond hair. "I love you, too, sweet girl."

Emotion squeezes my chest, and I am still reeling as I slip out of her room. I mean, I knew Tabby loved me, as I love her. But this is the first time she's spoken the words. I don't know why hearing the words said out loud is so much more poignant than knowing they're true.

I drift down the hall, tapping on Duke's bedroom door. It opens immediately. He folds me into his arms as he closes the door behind him. "I'm sorry. About Nan."

"No," I shake my head as I wrap my arms around him, surprised. "Duke, it's okay—"

"It's not," he insists, cutting me off. "It's just, I don't date. I'm not a person who has casual relationships." He leans back, his gaze burning into mine. "She knows that, and she can tell I care about you." His mouth opens like he's going to say more, but then he closes it, seeming to reconsider. After a pause, he says, "I reassured her that nothing with her relationship with Tabby would change with you in my life."

I study his face. With me in his life? As Tabby's nanny? As his lover? "Of course not. She's Tabby's grandmother. Tabby loves her."

He exhales, and it sounds like relief. "Exactly. That's what I tried to tell her." He pulls me against him again. "She asked if Tabby could spend some more time with her. Maybe some nights when I'm out of town, Tabby could sleep over there. Nan used to stay here, too, but I don't know how you would feel about that."

"She's welcome to stay here with Tabby." I'm sure I could stay with Lily on those nights. Violet mentioned during our lunch that she has a spare room. Maybe she would let me crash there sometimes, too.

"She asked if Tabby could sleep over tomorrow, while I'm out of town."

"Of course. She can pick her up off the bus. I bet Tabby would love that."

He smiles. "Great. I knew we could figure this all out." He sweeps me into his arms and carries me to the bed.

The kiss he gives me is sweet and slow. Then he trails his lips down my neck and over my breasts. We quickly remove our clothes, and I sigh when he presses his skin to mine. Whatever complications we might have or questions that remain unanswered, they aren't here, in this room. Everything about the way we move together is perfect.

When he comes inside me, I bury my hands in his hair, and we move together. I missed him more than I can explain, more than I want to even admit.

When I come undone around him, it strips me bare. I gasp his name as waves of pleasure shoot through me. He follows soon after, breathing heavily against my neck. We lie curled together, a tangle of limbs, in the aftermath.

After a quick trip to the bathroom, we fall back together on his bed sheets. He throws the comforter over us, and it sounds like he's fast asleep within moments of his head hitting the pillow.

I snuggle against him. I should tell him I'm a match to be a kidney donor for Lily. But until I can convince Lily to accept my kidney, it's still not a sure thing. There's no reason to add more to his plate until then. With Nancy willing to help again with Tabby while I have the procedure and during the immediate recovery, it's like all the pieces are falling into place.

He said he wants me to stay in his life. That means something, I hope. Because I care about him, and I want to stay in his and Tabby's lives too.

Duke

Hargreeves stops me when I get to the training facility the next day. "Duke, Raybourne wants to talk to you. Head up to the communications department before you take the ice."

I drop my gear at my locker and do as he says. When I knock on her door, Raybourne waves me in. "Pull that closed behind you, Duke." That doesn't sound good, but I do as she asks, trying to figure out what this is about. "Take a seat."

I slide into the chair in front of her, and she slips a folder across the desk. I open it. Inside is a picture of me holding June on the ice at the charity carnival. Behind it is another of me kissing her on the cheek. I set them down. "What's this?"

"It's an article I printed from one of the sports gossip rags. They published it this morning." She motions to the page behind the pictures. "Thought you should see it." She uses the eraser on her pencil to push it toward me.

On the paper is an article titled, "Who is June Harlow? All About the New Woman in Duke York's Life."

Something sours my stomach as I lift the page and read.

We spotted Duke York at the annual charity carnival, accompanied by his daughter and a stunning redhead. The official story is the woman with Duke is his daughter's nanny, June Harlow. But from what we saw (and based on these photos), there's more going on between Duke and his nanny than just childcare.

So who is June Harlow? Well, with a little sleuthing, we've discovered a few things about Duke's new mystery woman.

June Harlow is a former foster child. Her mother, Elizabeth Harlow, has prior arrests in both Camden and Burlington counties for possession, prostitution, and loitering. Since she was ten, she's lived with Lily Giancomo in Moorestown, NJ, and attended school there. She's held a handful of jobs around town through her teens. With the help of scholarships and student loans, she graduated from Rutgers in Camden in the spring. Her first proper job seems to be working with the captain of the Tyrants.

While her past reads like a rags-to-riches success story, things aren't sunshine and roses for Duke's new alleged love interest. She was recently spotted at a local pawnshop, selling off jewelry and china. No word on whose belongings they were.

Sure enough, there's a picture of June at this shop, smiling at the man behind the counter.

Unable to remain seated any longer, I spring to my feet, shaking the folder at Raybourne. "Who the hell writes this shit? Isn't it against the law to investigate people like this?"

Raybourne lifts her hands. "There's no proof someone found any of this information illegally. Did you finish the article?" She motions to my hands, where another piece of paper peeks out from under the picture of June at the pawnshop. I continue.

Perhaps the valuables belonged to Ms. Giancomo, who is undergoing expensive dialysis treatment. Like Miss Harlow, Ms. Giancomo is heavily in debt. She's behind on her medical bills, and her mortgage is in pre-foreclosure. We believe Miss Harlow plans to donate her own kidney to Ms. Giancomo. That may solve their problems, but if they need money, we wonder if Miss Harlow isn't banking on Duke York. We know Duke for his steady leadership and no-nonsense demeanor on the ice and off. But is it possible the steadfast captain of the Philadelphia Tyrants is falling victim to a pretty face and a sad tale, after claiming to want to avoid scandal this season? He wouldn't be the first wealthy man to fall prey to a gold digger. We would hate for him to be taken advantage of, but that kiss suggests something very personal is going on.

Stay tuned here for updates.

"This is disgusting." I drop the folder on Raybourne's desk. "But they're publishing information about Lily's health. That's definitely illegal." I pace back and forth in front of her desk.

"You can sue, of course," Raybourne says. "Though financially, that might not make sense. But what I need to know is if it's true."

"I already know about Lily, about the dialysis. I know about June being a foster kid, about her taking longer to finish college and needing to take out loans."

"That's not what I mean." She narrows her eyes at me. "Are you sleeping with June?"

I scowl at her. "What the hell does that have to do with anything?"

Raybourne presses her fingers to her forehead. "Oh, Duke. Of all the men on this team--"

"I love her."

She sighs and stands, rising to her imposing height in front of me. "I need you to stop to think for a moment." She motions to the chair in front of her again. "Please."

I do as she requests. When I'm settled, she sits again as well.

"We need to look at this without emotion," she says. That anyone is lecturing me about being rational is pretty funny. "You know what happened last year with Hammond. He was married, but sex scandals are like crack to these people."

Hammond was the guy who had the affair and ended up in a messy divorce last year. "This isn't a sex scandal. It's a relationship. I love her."

Raybourne's brows lift. "Fine. So all of this is true? And you knew about it? The financial problems and the kidney donation?"

"I didn't know about the late payments. And a kidney donation..." My voice trails off. That's got to be bullshit. I hate that some ugly article is making me doubt her. "I trust June. She's no gold digger. I'm sure there are explanations for all of this."

"I'm not suggesting you shouldn't trust her," Raybourne says calmly. "In fact, all of my instincts say she's trustworthy, too. But you need to be aware of the situation. You're a successful athlete with a lot of money. It will naturally draw people to you, and people who write these—" she points to the article, "—things will naturally be suspicious."

I lean back in my chair, feeling the weight of her words sink in. It's true that June hasn't been open with me about her financial struggles, but none of what Raybourne is saying fits what I know about June. I shake my head. "It's just that when we started..." I pause. "When our relationship got more serious, she told me she wouldn't accept my paycheck any longer. She wouldn't do that if it was only about money."

"True. But that doesn't seem practical. How does she plan to pay her bills?" Raybourne asks.

"She mentioned a substitute teaching position. I assumed she had savings or something until she found something."

I can only blink at Raybourne. She's right—I didn't know the extent of June or Lily's financial problems. And a pawnshop? People only pawn things if they're really struggling. Was she going to pawn shops to make ends meet? But she didn't say anything to me. What was she pawning, and why?

Not to mention the talk of kidney donations. Was that just made-up bullshit or is there some truth to that?

I don't care that June has financial problems. She's twenty-four and right out of college. There are lots of recent graduates—too many—who struggle with debt. But I don't know why she kept all of this to herself. The secrets... they stir up ancient hurts.

When Sonya started having headaches during her third trimester, she said it was probably because of hormone fluctuations. She would get occasional migraines before her periods, and she assumed it was something like that. But when they got worse and caused her to throw up, I worried. She waved me off. She kept going to her obstetric appointments, and Tabby was great, healthy and perfectly normal. Then she had a seizure, and I rushed her to the emergency room.

She had a brain tumor. Glioblastoma. It was aggressive. The doctors suggested surgery, followed by chemotherapy and radiation. She was thirty weeks. She agreed to the surgery but postponed chemotherapy and radiation for five weeks until Tabby's lungs were prepared for her to be born. I tried to convince her to be more aggressive and to start treatments right away. The doctors told her a body of research supported starting her treatment during pregnancy. They said she was in her third trimester, and it was generally regarded as low-risk. But Sonya wouldn't hear it. She had read the research, too, especially the statistics for how long someone with her condition was expected to live. In her mind, her chances weren't great, no matter what. She waited.

At thirty-five weeks, the doctor induced her. Tabby was born perfect, and Sonya started treatments immediately. But she only lived for a couple of months, anyway.

I don't know if she would have lived longer if she'd made different choices. All I know is how helpless I felt in those months. There weren't any good options. Her prognosis for survival was bad. That didn't make the heartbreak any easier.

Over the years, I've wondered if she suspected she was sick. Sonya was a smart woman. She had to have guessed something was wrong. If she had, she kept it from me. I'll never know, and it doesn't change the past. It's the doubts, though. They nag at me, make me believe my wife had kept secrets from me. Lied.

But this is different. These are June's private financial affairs. Maybe she is embarrassed. Maybe she's afraid I would think less of her. I'm upset she didn't trust me with it, but this isn't something insurmountable. The kidney thing... I'm sure they're making shit up.

It has to be different.

Raybourne glares at me from across the desk. "Seriously, Duke. Did you consider how it would look if you got caught sleeping with your nanny? We talked about this. Now with this,"—she motions to the article— "have you considered how this makes you look? If this angle—that she's looking for money—doesn't work, they can spin it in other ways, you know. They can say you're her boss, taking advantage of her situation. A younger girl with no money, wowed by her rich employer. Have you thought about that?"

I hadn't. "Why does anyone think they can be involved in my personal business?" I growl out.

"Because you're the captain of a professional hockey team. The same captain who is on record multiple times last year reprimanding your teammates for their behavior."

"That was different," I exclaim. "I never talked about my teammates' private lives. I'm a professional, and I kept things about business—how they behaved on the ice, how they treated each other in the locker room."

"I know. But that won't keep the gossips out of your personal life now. You need to talk to her," Raybourne tells me, pushing the article across the table. "We need to know what's going on with her, so we can craft a response."

Raybourne has good intentions, but I hate that she's in my business. Craft a response. Like I'm a fire she's putting out.

I get it, though. She's just doing her job. I take a deep breath and nod. But as I leave Raybourne's office, my mind spins.

I check my watch. I need to be on the ice in ten minutes, so I pick up my pace. Once the morning drills finish, I'll see if I can catch June before Tabby gets home, straighten this all out. Then Raybourne can craft her response, and we'll move on.

June

I don't waste any time talking with Lily about the transplant. When I pick her up for dialysis the next morning, I blurt it as soon as she's settled in the car. "I'm a match. You're getting a new kidney."

"No."

I keep talking like she said nothing. "I called the scheduler before I left the house. We'll go in on Tuesday for pre-op testing, and then the procedure will be Friday. They did most of my testing when I was in originally, but they need to make sure nothing has changed."

"In one week?" Lily shakes her head. "June—"

I take a deep breath and go for the grand finale. "It's yours," I tell her. "This is my gift to you."

Lily looks out the window. I wait in silence while she works through her thoughts. "The risks..." she finally says, her voice trailing off.

I squeeze her hand and briefly meet her eyes as I steer into the dialysis center parking lot. "It will save you from having to go through dialysis. Your insurance isn't covering enough of it, not if you want to keep the house." I motion to the building. "Once this is done, you'll get another chance. You can heal up. Move back home." I turn off the car, facing her. Squeezing her hand, I stare at her. "This is a common procedure. Doctors do lots of kidney transplants."

She squeezes my hand. "Are you sure about this?" Her eyes narrow, and her grip is steel. "Really sure? This is a huge decision you're making."

"I'm certain. It's all I've been thinking about."

She searches my face. I'm not sure what answer she's trying to find, so I wait. Finally, she nods. "All right. We'll do it. But I'll never be able to thank you enough." Her voice shakes with emotion.

"I love you, Lily." I lean forward to squeeze her.

"I love you back, sweet girl," she whispers.

After her dialysis, I drive Lily home. I leave my phone in the car as I help her in. When I get back and buckle up, I check it. There's a message from Violet.

You need to see this. She sent a link, too, and I click.

There's a picture of me at the pawnshop. I'm standing at the front counter, speaking with the clerk, Tex. I learned his name the second time I went in to ask him how much he might give me for Lily's antique sewing machine. This must have been the time I sold some of her mother's jewelry. Lily didn't even want to see the jewelry before I sold it, said it would be too painful.

A quick skim of the link reveals another picture. It's Duke kissing me at the charity event. I suck in a quick breath.

Scrolling to the top, I begin the article under the pawnshop photograph and go icy cold. I grew up poor, the daughter of an addict, and I've been called a lot of names in my life, but this word salad of an article takes the cake.

My heart pounds as I read it through, but I don't get the full idea of it because my mind keeps snagging on new and painful insinuations. A gold digger, that's what it calls me. A girl who fell into a sweet situation and is eager to capitalize. Duke is my victim, a widower who fell for a pretty face. Someone I'm trying to get to fix all my problems. I'm manipulative and greedy.

I reread it, and this time I pause on my mother's name. Prostitution. I squeeze my eyes closed, but the word is still there, I'm sure. It's not a surprise. I always suspected, but seeing it printed is mortifying. Shame whips at my stomach, making me nauseous. I swallow hard and keep reading.

Lily. It talks about Lily, brings up her financial problems. Anger flares, wiping out my self-pity, and I welcome it. How dare they talk about Lily like that?

As I continue to scroll, stewing in a toxic mix of shame and fury, I stop at the mention of the kidney donation. I drop my phone into my lap to stare out the window like the answers to all of my problems are out there.

Did Duke see this yet? I wince. Probably. If Violet forwarded it to me, it's probably common knowledge. Or, if it isn't, it's about him, so he'll find out. But I don't have any messages from him. The team had practice today, before they leave tomorrow for another stretch of away games, so maybe he hadn't had a second away.

This isn't how I hoped to tell him about my kidney surgery, but I guess I can't change that now.

Starting the car, I drive home, my brain attempting to do damage control. Tabby's too young to see the article, but will Tabby's school see it? If Ms. Shepherd planned to recommend me for the substitute position, I bet the article will make her think twice.

I'm sure Duke and I can come up with a way to smooth this over. Last night, he said this thing between us isn't casual. He cares about me, and I care about him. That article might make it seem dirty, but it isn't. Not to me, and hopefully not to him.

I'll need to move out, though. If we're going to continue to see each other, I can't live with him and Tabby. It's inappropriate, especially now with this article airing everything. These public conversations are exactly what the communication director warned against when I got hired. I don't even want to think about how they might affect Tabby. I can probably stay with Lily for a day or so, but then I'll need to find somewhere else to live. Violet mentioned she's got a spare room. Maybe she'd agree to a roommate.

My head spins as I turn onto our street. Duke's car is parked out front, and I pull in next to it. He's not supposed to be home until dinnertime. My stomach swirls. He must have seen the article. Well, best to tackle head on. "Duke," I call, throwing open the side door. "Are you here?"

"I'm in the living room," he responds, and I follow the sound of his voice. I find him staring out the window at the pool.

"Hey." I pull my crossbody bag over my head. "I assume you're home because of the article."

Turning, he nods. His face is grim. "Raybourne pulled me in this morning."

That was her name. Ms. Raybourne, the head of the communications department. Not good. "I see." I inhale a steadying breath. "What are we going to do?"

He waits. Finally, he asks, "Is any of it true?"

I still, and the question hits me in the middle of the chest, like a physical blow. "What?"

"The article. Is any of that stuff true?"

I can only blink at him. When I walked in the door, I figured we would work through this together. If I'm important to him, if we're a couple, then that's what we would do—take on obstacles as a team.

But as I stare at him, I realize this isn't a working partnership—this is an interrogation.

I hoped for so much more, and now, staring at his guarded face, I realize how naïve that was. "The part about me being a manipulative gold digger? Or the assumption that I'm taking advantage of Tabby to get close to you?" I cross my arms over my chest. "There's so much to unpack."

He rakes his hands through his hair. "Shit, June..." He exhales like he's exasperated—like he's the one who's facing accusations here. "This seems like a huge thing in your life. Why didn't you say something to me?"

"Because we don't talk about money." I open my arms to include the beautiful home around me. "Look at this place. You had someone come in to install bookshelves in the playroom and you didn't blink an eye. Complaining to you about money would have been weird."

His hands settle on his hips. "June... I thought we were..." He trails off, and then his jaw firms. "This isn't just regular financial struggles. You went to the pawnshop."

I want to bristle at the hint of accusation I hear in his tone, but I hold my expression neutral. "Yes. I went to a pawnshop. I sold some things for Lily. I didn't realize I needed to run that by you."

"Is she okay? Financially, I mean?"

"No." I narrow my eyes at him. "I wouldn't be selling her things if she was okay." As I watch the confusion play over his features, I realize he wouldn't understand how it feels to be financially unstable. Hockey is an expensive sport to play, so he must have grown up in comfort. Then he signed to a huge contract early on. The gap in our experiences widens.

"Can I help her?"

I shake my head. "She won't take money from you. She's not a charity case."

"But she would accept it from you. Why didn't you ask me for help?"

"Because of this." I wave my hand to encompass him. "The pity on your face is bad enough. I wasn't just going to ask to borrow some money. We're not just friends. Besides, until recently, you paid all of my bills. The only reason you stopped paying me is because we're sleeping together, and I refused my salary."

His expression closes further, and he folds his arms over his chest. "We're sleeping together. Is that all?"

I've hurt him, but I'm hurting, too. "You tell me, Duke. What exactly are we? Last night, you introduced me as your nanny to Nancy. I live here. I take care of Tabby, and we sleep together." These are the facts, and they're what I have. I've never had the luxury to pretend my reality differed from what it was. It would be easy for me to romanticize it. I've never felt like this about anyone before. It hurts to even imagine my life without them. But that doesn't change the facts.

He sweeps forward and grips my shoulders. He's not rough, but his eyes are intense as they stare into mine. "I love you. That's what we are."

The words drop like a cannonball in his living room. It's only after they're in the air that I realize how much I've been dreaming of hearing them.

These past weeks haven't only been great—they've been magical for me. A fairy tale. Duke's an amazing lover, sure, but it's so much more than that. I've been able to pretend we're a little family, and it's everything I've ever wanted. I wanted him and his daughter to be mine, more than I've wanted anything else before.

But not like this.

"You love me," I repeat, shaking my head. "Then how can you believe any of the garbage in that article? It says I'm using you, that I'm a gold digger. Worse, that I'm using Tabby." Even saying the words makes me feel sick.

He blows out a frustrated breath. "Hell, June. I don't believe that shit. No way. But all these secrets." He shakes his head. "I don't understand."

"Secrets? They're not secrets. This is my life." How would he understand any of that? But even if he doesn't, I should have. I should have seen how I wouldn't fit into his world here. I press my hand to my forehead. "I'll need to move out. I should have before, when we started sleeping together." I just didn't want to. I've been too caught up in the fairy tale of being here with him. Spending the nights in his bed, dinners together. Being around to hear all of Tabby's ramblings when she gets home from school. Even considering leaving hurts my heart.

"Wait, why?"

"Because it's not appropriate for me to live here with your daughter. It's exactly what Ms. Raybourne warned us about in the beginning. You'll still need someone to help with Tabby, of course. I'll still be able to do that. I'll still be able to do that, even after." Talking things out has always helped me work through problems. My brain races with the added complication of caring for Tabby when I'm not living here. "Now that Nancy is getting better, she can take some nights, especially after my surgery."

"What surgery?" Duke interrupts me, his tone clipped.

I glance up at him and register the panic on his face. "The transplant surgery." This wasn't how I planned to tell him, but we'll need to work it into the schedule now, if Tabby won't be affected. "I'm donating my kidney to Lily."

"You're donating a kidney. Like it says in the article." I should be used to him repeating statements like questions.

"Yes. I found out last night I'm a match. They referred us to a specialist for the procedure."

"I see." His face says he clearly doesn't. "You've decided to donate a kidney, and I didn't know. When did you plan to tell me?" It's impossible to miss the betrayal in his tone, and it unsettles me.

I lift my shoulders helplessly. "Today. I planned to tell you today. I wanted to talk to Lily first, to make sure she understood and agreed."

"She didn't agree?" He rubs his temple. "Didn't you think this was something I should have known about? A kidney donation is major surgery."

"I told you. I wasn't sure Lily was on board until this morning. I didn't think it was worth discussing until I was sure. But it seems like everything is falling together. Nancy can take care of Tabby while I'm recovering. So there shouldn't be a major disruption for you at all."

He blinks at me, his jaw working. "It's not about the childcare. It's about you," he grits out.

"What?"

"I can find other childcare. I can't find another you." He enunciates every word like I don't speak English. Then he buries his hands in his hair and paces the length of the room. "Christ, June. How is it possible I've lived with you—that I'm in love with you—and I don't know any of this? I can't imagine how we can make anything work between us if you can't share what's important with me."

"Duke..." He looks lost, and I don't know what to say to him.

He shakes his head. "I need to get back to the training center. We leave for Boston in an hour. We can...talk about this more later. Don't forget that Nancy asked to take Tabby tonight. She'll be here when Tabby gets off the bus." He picks up his jacket, already heading for the door. Retreating. "I'll see you tomorrow night when I get back."

The sound of the door closing behind him is like a thunderclap. I'm rooted to the spot in the living room, staring after him.

That couldn't have gone worse. I drop onto the couch, covering my face with my hands. That article points out everything I've suspected. I don't fit here with Duke. He's successful and rich, and he has a daughter to raise. Me? I'm a walking financial deficit, the daughter of a whore with no experience in relationships. I've seen them done in movies and read about it all in books, but I didn't have any close role models. My mom had flings, not even actual relationships, and she never married.

Honestly, besides Lily, no one has ever made a place for me. If I was him, I don't know that I'd take a chance on me. Maybe he doesn't see what a risk I am, but I can see it. That article was exactly the reminder I needed.

Tabby is staying with Nancy tonight, so she doesn't need me. That's good. I can use this time to figure out where I can go. I can probably stay with Lily for a couple of days, but I need a more permanent solution.

For now, though... I reach into my pocket and text Violet. *Any chance you're around tonight? I could use a place to crash.*

―ℓℓ―

"Thank you for letting me stay here," I tell Violet later as I drag my suitcase into the hall of her apartment in Philadelphia. It's a second-floor walkup, but it's downtown, right near all the clubs and restaurants.

"No problem. Like I told you earlier, I have a spare room. You can stay as long as you want." Violet looks chic in jogger sweats and an oversized cropped sweatshirt. Her socks have tiny pink hearts on them, and she makes even them look effortlessly elegant.

"I wasn't sure if you were looking for a roommate, but as soon as I get a job, I'll be able to pay rent. It shouldn't be more than a couple of weeks." The surgery might set me back a week or so, but after that, I'll be ready.

Violet waves a hand at me. "It's not a big deal. My father actually footed the first six months for me. I told him I could make my way, but I'm from Texas and a long way from home. I think it made him feel better to take care of me." Like always, Violet delivers this information with a breeziness I can't imagine. As if a family member spotting her thousands of dollars is no big deal at all. I can't imagine that kind of caretaking. "But what happened to your old job? With Duke?"

I set my suitcase on its wheels. It's busted, though, so it falls. I prop it against the wall. "Well, jobs get complicated when you sleep with your boss." I sigh. When I say the words out loud, it sounds cheap.

Violet gasps and squeals. "I knew it. I told Hunter, but he was sure Duke wouldn't do that. But I can always guess."

My cheeks are on fire. "It's actually... complicated."

"You said."

"He has Tabby."

"Hence the job," she points out.

"Right," I allow. "Well, I won't say all the things about Tabby, but she needs me. But my foster mother, Lily, is in kidney failure. She needs me, too." I inhale and breathe out slowly. "I'm going to give her one of my kidneys."

Violet lifts her hands. "Hold on. You're not wrong. This is complicated." She heads into the tiny kitchen and pulls a bottle of wine out of her refrigerator. "I think you need to start from the beginning, and I have just the thing for a story like this."

I've only known Violet for a month, but during that time, I've come to value her friendship. I trust her.

She pours us both very healthy glasses, and we take them into the open space that doubles as a dining room and a living room. I sit on the couch, tuck my feet under me, and spill my guts. I tell her about my mother, about entering the foster system and meeting Lily. I explain how I've worked so hard to get through college, all the jobs, all the ways I worked to improve myself. I allude to Lily's finances, but I don't feel comfortable saying much about Lily's private business. I do tell her about the kidney dialysis, about the costs and about her declining prognosis.

"I'm so sorry," Violet says, gripping my hand.

"Thank you." I squeeze back. "But it's going to be okay. They think that she'll have a full life with a new kidney."

"And you're a match."

"Yes." I sit up straighter. "I'm so glad I can do this for her."

"That's an enormous gift you're giving her." Violet reaches for her wineglass. "I'm sure she appreciates what you're doing."

"It's nothing compared to what she did for me. She took me in, raised me."

"Yes, but it sounds like you've been a great daughter to her, too."

"I guess—"

"And you've thought through all the risks involved?" She lifts her eyebrows as she sips.

"Of course. No contact sports. That's no loss. I sing as well as I play sports." Violet freezes across from me, and I laugh at her. "Please. I'm well aware I stink. But I should be able to live a full and healthy life without my other kidney ."

She smiles at me. "You're a really good person, June Harlow."

I wave her off. "Anyone would do it for someone they love."

"Maybe. But it's just one example. Like Tabby. You're talking about how you basically broke up with Duke, but you're worried he won't have someone to take care of Tabby." She toasts me. "Trust me. After breakups, most girls aren't worrying about what they can do for their exes."

Is that what Duke and I are now, exes? That leaves an aching hole in my stomach, an empty space that feels wrong. "She needs my help. He does, too."

"Maybe. But what do you need?" She tilts her head. Her gaze is assessing. Though Violet puts on the facade of serene beauty and fun, she's much more discerning than people probably guess. "You're worrying about everyone else. Like a goddamned saint. But what do you need?"

I shift, uncomfortable. Compliments and personal questions make me squirmy. I shrug. "I mean, what everyone needs, I guess. Food. A place to stay. Stuff like that."

"Those are basic needs." She scowls at me. "I mean, what is it you want, June? Out of your life, I mean?" She empties her wine glass. "You've spent your whole life reacting. To your mother, the foster system, even your own financial situation. Now, this situation with Duke. It sounds like you're in constant triage. But if you could choose, what would you want?"

I open my mouth, but I don't have a response. These aren't things I've let myself think about. "I don't know," I finally say.

"Well," she stands. "While you think about it, I think we need more wine." She tips her glass at me and heads for the galley kitchen.

Unsettled, I follow. "Maybe I would like just a little more."

Duke

It's a short flight to Boston, but it does nothing to soothe the chaos in my head. I sit next to Huck, but he must read on my face that I'm not interested in talking.

I spent all afternoon thinking about how June and I left our conversation. With some distance, I admit she's right about some of it. People are different in how they approach their finances. When she accused me of being blasé about mine, she was right. I've never had to worry about money. But I'm in the minority, and it was a dickhead move to forget that.

Do I wish she could have been more open about her financial problems? Yes. I can probably understand that, though. But the surgery... I still don't understand why she didn't tell me, and I'm struggling to let it go.

After I get checked in at the hotel and drop my bag in my room, I try to relax. We have a one-o'clock game tomorrow afternoon, so I need to get some sleep. But I can't settle, so I head down to the lobby. I don't know where I plan to go, but I know I need a walk.

Huck's staring into a coffee cup at the bar. I join him, sliding onto the stool beside him. Exhaling, I wave to the bartender. "Angel's Envy on the rocks."

Huck hums in response. "Bourbon on a school night, huh?"

I accept the drink, turning it around in my hand. "I screwed up."

He lifts his mug—which appears to be some kind of tea—and holds it out to me. I toast with him and take a gulp that burns on the way down. "What did you screw up?"

I tell him everything—about the article and my conversation with June. I spill the jumble of thoughts that have been spinning in my head since I found out about how she's helping Lily. He listens quietly and then sips his drink.

"You did mess up," he admits.

I glare at him. "That's not helpful."

"Oh, you wanted help?" He rolls his eyes. "That's not what you said."

I sigh. "Fuck..."

"Maybe it's not that you screwed up. You overreacted, right after you flinched. That's what you did." He shrugs.

"Flinched? I don't flinch." I'm a professional hockey player.

"You love her. But she's planned something you disagree with. This is the first time you guys have disagreed, right?"

"We disagree lots." That's not entirely untrue. June and I debate a lot of things. Disagreement might be too strong for those conversations. "This is the first important thing, yes."

"And it sounds like you panicked."

"I wouldn't say panic...."

"Panic. She's planning to have surgery, did it without you, and scared the shit out of you." He points at me with his mug. "Flashbacks and panic."

I don't know what to say. I sit there with my mouth open, speechless.

"Sonya. She did that to you." When I only stare at him, he continues with a shrug. "You forget how long I've known you. I remember after Sonya died, don't forget. I remember the dark times, how you second-guessed everything. Your choices, her choices. But June isn't Sonya. You can't treat her like she is."

"I just...." I drop my elbows on the bar and bury my hands in my hair. "I can't do something like that again." Losing Sonya almost broke me, and I had felt completely powerless. Listening to June tell me today about how this was her decision...those memories almost made me sick. "I can't lose June."

"There's no guarantee you won't. It's a surgery, and I get being afraid. Stuff like that's scary. But it sounds like you might have pushed her away—lost her—already." He isn't unkind, but he's firm. "You're a great hockey captain. You're a wonderful father. But you can't control everything. And you shouldn't want to control the ones you care about."

Is that what I was doing? Not intentionally, and not control exactly. It's part of who I am to protect the people I love. Sonya and June.... They purposely put themselves in harm's way. How can I protect June from an elective kidney transplant, after all?

"You don't know what June is going through. How much do you really know about her background, about her life? And you busted into it, making judgments. Instead of asking her how she felt and what was going on, you reacted. That's how you screwed up."

I drop my head. Fuck. He's right. I pushed her away—the best thing that's happened to me in a really long time—because I was too afraid of feeling helpless again, of getting hurt. I didn't just screw up. I fucked this up completely.

I down the rest of my drink and stand. Smacking Huck on the back, I point to his tea. "Don't be too long. We have shit to do tomorrow."

He gives me a mock salute. "Aye, aye."

I head back to the stairwell, taking the steps two at a time up to the second floor. Before I can talk myself out of it, I dial June's number on my phone. But she doesn't answer. I frown as I drop into her voicemail.

After the voicemail prompt, I take a breath and say, "June. I'm sorry. I messed everything up. Please, call me back." I debate telling her I love her, but I don't. "Talk to you soon."

I hang up and stare at the phone in my hand. Kicking off my shoes, I head into the bathroom and splash water on my face before I brush my teeth. The minutes stretch on, and she doesn't return my call. I tell myself it's late, maybe she's asleep already.

Setting the phone on my nightstand, I strip off my clothes and collapse into bed. Before I turn off the light, I make sure the phone isn't on mute. After that, I lay in the darkness and listen for the phone ringing, but it never does.

The night drags on, and I don't hear from her. Part of me wants to call again, beg if I need to. Eventually, I drift off into an uneasy sleep.

In the morning, I wake up early, but I don't feel rested at all. I check my phone. No calls or texts. Unable to stop myself, I pull up a text message. *Hey. I'm so sorry. I miss you. Please call me back.*

The typing dots appear and stay there for long moments. I wait. Finally, they disappear. After a moment, they start again. When her response appears, it's short. *Nancy is keeping Tabby until you get home. But I'll be there on Monday to get Tabby on the bus.*

I stare at the words. So many replies sift through my head. But if she wanted to hear my apology or to talk more, she would have called back. From this, though, it sounds like she still wants to be part of our lives. For now, that means something. *Tabby would love that*, I reply, because she doesn't seem ready to hear what I love.

I try not to get discouraged, but I can't help thinking I've lost my chance with her.

June

According to Duke's schedule, he flew home from Boston on Saturday night. There's nothing on our joint calendar for Sunday, but he needs to be at the training center early on Monday. I text him Sunday night to tell him I'll be at his house by six o'clock to get Tabby ready for school and on the bus.

I use my key to let myself in, not wanting to wake Tabby. From the door, I can see Duke sitting at the island in the kitchen, so I join him. Best to tackle this head-on.

"Hey," I tell him, bracing myself.

"Hey," he responds, standing. I get my first look at him in a few days, and I hate how even the sight of him makes my chest lighter. There are dark smudges under his eyes, though. He must be sleeping as badly as I am. He runs his hand through his hair. "Listen, June..."

"Wait." I hold up my hand. "First, I need to say something." I inhale. "You were probably right. I should have told you about the surgery, especially because you were relying on me to care for Tabby." Even two days later, the words in that article, about how I was using them, still stung.

"It's not about Tabby." He sighs. I feel like he wants to reach for me. He opens his hand, but at the last moment, he drops it to his side. "June, I fucked up."

I shake my head. "No—"

"Yes. The way I reacted on Friday, that's my baggage." He sighs and swallows hard. "Sonya died of glioblastoma. A brain tumor. They found it when she was pregnant with Tabby. She didn't want to do any treatment, not until after Tabby was born, afraid of how it might affect her. There's research about the negative effects of chemotherapy and radiation on babies in utero and...." His voice trails off. "Well, we disagreed on how her treatment should have proceeded."

He runs a hand over his face. "Do you know how hard it is to be angry with someone you love so much, to feel like they're not taking care of themselves? I wanted to respect her wishes, but I disagreed with her choices and there was nothing I could do about it. I loved that she was protecting Tabby. But I hated she wasn't choosing herself. I was so afraid of losing her, of losing Tabby. It paralyzed me." He exhales. "It was a shit situation, and I felt helpless. Worse than helpless. I felt useless." He shrugs. "That's the first time I think I've ever said any of that."

My throat is tight with tears. Duke is so protective and stoic. I can't imagine how much it must have broken him to lose her like that. For the first time, I glimpse how much he must care about me, to tell me these things.

"When you told me about the transplant, I ended up back in that place, in those days. It wasn't fair, and you're completely right. You need to do what you feel is right, and helping Lily is so brave and strong... like you."

My throat tightens, and I squeeze his hand. "I'm going to be okay," I say because I can't stand the panic I see in his eyes. "They told me everything will be okay."

He nods. "I know they did. I'm sure they're right." He says the words, but I can tell he doesn't believe them. I tilt my head, understanding him a little better. After all, it's one thing to know logically, but sometimes emotions aren't logical. "What I'm trying to tell you, all of this... I want to be with you. I love you, June. And loving someone means loving them through hard times and choices, even if you're afraid."

If my heart hurt before, his words tighten my chest further, making it difficult to breathe. Every part of me wants to believe him, to lean forward into his arms. I want to tell him I love him, too, because I'm sure that I do. But none of that changes anything between us.

"Duke," I start. "Thank you. I appreciate you saying all that. I do. But I don't think you were wrong before. How can you be with someone who can't tell you important things?"

Duke's eyebrows drop. "Can you explain to me how you're getting where you are right now, after everything I just said?"

"I mean, I didn't tell you important stuff. I suck at this, and I'm going to keep screwing up." I tuck one hand on my hip and press the other against my forehead. "It's clear you've been through some hard things. You've lost so much already, you and Tabby. And I'm just saying that I'm not a good bet. I mean, I don't know how to be in a relationship. I'm twenty-four, and this is the closest I've come to one. My mom... well, let's just say she wasn't a great role model. And you have that precious girl." I point upstairs. "I don't know how to do this."

"June. Stop." He reaches for me, and I step back.

"How will you ever know that stuff in that article isn't true?" I ask, and I hate how broken my voice sounds.

"Because I know you. And we can figure the rest of this out together. I know we can."

"And I don't know that." I turn from him, pressing my fingers into my temple. It's so tempting, what he's offering. But that article and the way he responded just showed me how much I have to lose if I put faith in anyone but myself. "You have practice. You should go."

"June, please." It's a plea, and I swear, it physically hurts me. "Don't do this."

When I face him, I fold my arms around my waist, as if I can somehow shield myself from the pain inside me. "I'll see you later, Duke."

He stands, his hands at his side, searching my face. As I watch, he clenches his fists and then loosens them slowly. Finally, he lets out an unsteady breath and shakes his head. "If that's what you want." He moves toward the door and picks up his workout bag. "But I never pictured you for a quitter."

He slings the bag over his shoulder and leaves. The door into the garage closes softly behind him.

Duke

THE NEXT THREE DAYS are hellish. Instead of texting me, June goes directly to Nancy to coordinate childcare coverage for Tabby. It's more efficient, but it takes away any reason for me to communicate with June. I only get to see her a few times in passing, and all those interactions are courteous and professional. I hate them.

Nancy's car is in the driveway when I return home on Thursday night. As I step through the door from the garage, something smells delicious. Tabby comes running from the living room, cradling a doll in her arms. I swing her up into a hug, and she tells me about the game she's playing. I kiss her cheek, and I tell her to go wash up before dinner.

After she scurries off, I lift my eyebrows at Nancy, who's sitting at the island, reading a book. "I assume June left dinner?"

Nancy points to the slow cooker. "Some Tuscan dish."

I glance in. Seems like something with tomatoes and chicken. It smells even better up close. I sigh.

"What's going on with you two, anyway?" Nancy closes her book and props her elbow on the island.

"What do you mean?" I ask, buying for time.

"She texts me to schedule. She doesn't live here anymore." Her eyebrows lift. "She looks about as miserable and tired as you do. Something is going on."

I can't stop thinking about the uncertainty in June's eyes on Monday morning when we last talked about our relationship. It was as if an invisible barrier had gone up between us. I understand she is afraid, and the way I behaved last week about the article and her donation to Lily didn't help. But nothing has gotten easier this week. I miss her, and I don't know how to get through to her.

I try to think of something to say. "It's complicated."

"Uncomplicate it."

I exhale in frustration. "Don't you think I want to?" This entire week, I've tried to figure out what I can say to get through to her, but all I keep remembering is the finality in her voice.

Nancy stares at me, waiting. Finally, she presses her palms against the island in front of her. "She won't be able to help with Tabby this next week. Did you know that?" I offer her a quick nod. "Did you know why?"

I swallow. "She's having surgery. Donating her kidney to her foster mother."

Nancy inhales sharply, and her eyes narrow on me. "Does that have something to do with what's going on between you two?"

I close my eyes, rubbing my forehead. "No. Yes. Sort of."

"That clears it up."

"I might have panicked when I found out."

"Because of what Sonya went through? Her medical problems?" Her brows have lifted.

"Not exactly." I shrug. "June didn't tell me. About the surgery. And I felt like she kept secrets."

Nancy's eyes widen with recognition. "Ah. Like Sonya did."

I slide onto the island stool across from her. "Like Sonya."

She covers my hand. "You know, I didn't agree with how my daughter managed her illness." I nod. We've talked about this many times. "But I understand it, and that's the most important part." I tilt my head in question. "You won't agree with someone—even someone you love—about everything. That isn't the point. It's our job, when we love someone, to try to understand them. To know them."

I scowl at her. "Of course, I understand why June's doing this. It's brave, generous. Amazing, even."

"The actual donation isn't the part you might not be getting." Her voice is gentle. "Do you understand why she might not have told you?"

I exhale heavily. "No. I don't." When Nancy waits, I continue. "She hasn't had an easy start."

"Has she talked with you about that? About how she grew up?"

"A bit. She doesn't like to talk about herself much."

"Then ask yourself this," Nancy continues. "What did she go through that makes it hard for her to open up to you?" She stands, patting my hand again. "Her surgery is tomorrow. If you decide you want to change your schedule, just let me know. I'm around all day."

I sit at the kitchen island, staring at the slow cooker. Nancy's words echo in my head, asking me to understand June. She's right, of course. I should have been more understanding. I know firsthand how hard it is to open up about personal struggles. After Sonya died, I retreated into myself. Though I don't know all the details about June's life, the things I know are sad, even heartbreaking.

I should have been there for June when she needed me. I don't know what to do or how to make it right. But I know I can't let June go through this alone. Not after everything she's done for me.

Grabbing my phone out of my pocket, I type out a message to June, my thumbs moving quickly over the screen. *I'm thinking of you, and I'm here for you. Whatever you need. I want to be there for you if you'll let me.*

I hesitate for a moment, staring at the message. Is it too much? Not enough? I don't know, but it's a start. I take a deep breath and hit send. Almost immediately, my phone buzzes with a response from June.

Thank you. I appreciate your support right now.

I read her message. It's not just thoughts and words I want to give her. I want to help, to be there for her during her surgery and recovery. I know it won't be easy, but I'm willing to do whatever it takes to make things right between us. Because I know one thing for sure: I love her, and I don't want to lose her.

June

I SLEEP ON THE couch at Lily's apartment on Thursday, the night before our surgery. We're supposed to check in tomorrow morning at six o'clock, so I figured it would be easier to just leave from here instead of coming from Violet's in the city.

But apparently, Lily's couch has the most uncomfortable cushions ever created. Either that's keeping me awake, or it's the text from Duke.

Shifting to my other side, I tuck my hands under my head. This week has been brutal without him. It's worse because I've seen him, but I force myself to pretend like nothing happened between us. Like I don't love him. I try to remind myself of all the reasons things can't work. He's my boss—was my boss. We are from completely different backgrounds. I was the subject of a gossip article about him and the reason he got called into the communication department. That's even before I consider that I have no idea how to be in a healthy relationship.

I should have talked with him. I don't even understand why I didn't. Why couldn't I open up to him the way I opened up to Violet? It should have been that easy. But I couldn't.

Shifting again, I jab at my pillow in irritation.

"What did that pillow do to you?"

I stretch up to see Lily in the door of her bedroom. "I'm sorry. Am I keeping you awake?" Immediately, I feel guilty. We're having surgery tomorrow. We need to sleep.

She shakes her head, turning on the light next to the couch. "No. Can't turn my brain off. You?"

I scoot to sit. "Same." I pat the couch next to me, and she joins me.

"You worrying about the procedure?" she asks. "Because there's still time to call it off."

"Absolutely not." I squeeze her hand. "That's not what's on my mind."

"Ah." She nods knowingly. "Duke, then." I'd filled Lily in on my breakup with Duke. She had listened, but if she had any suggestions, she kept them to herself.

"Yeah."

We sit in silence for long moments, lost in thought. Finally, Lily encircles my arm with hers. "You know, June, you've always been a good girl."

This is a strange change of subject, but I don't really want to talk about Duke. So I pat her hand, smiling. "Thanks, Mama."

"No, I mean it. I've fostered a lot of children over the years, but you were always the easiest." She shakes her head. "Straight As in school. Sunshiny personality. Always helpful, with the other kids and with the neighborhood."

I lay my head on her shoulder. "I didn't want to cause you any problems."

"I know, hon." She squeezes my head in a sideways hug. "And it helped me, so I didn't question you. But even the best kids have some sort of rebellion. Something. Not you, though."

She falls silent. In the quiet, I shift, uncomfortable. "That's not a bad thing, right?"

"Of course not. But I hated to see you so afraid."

I sit up straight. "Afraid?"

"Since the moment you arrived, you were afraid I'd kick you out."

I shake my head. "No, no. It wasn't like that."

"It was exactly like that." She pats my arm again.

Her words settle in my stomach. *Afraid*. I never really thought it was fear. I just knew if I was easy to live with, easy to be around, that maybe I wouldn't be left behind again. People like easy people. So I did my best to be likable.

"I love you, Junie. And I would have loved you even if you rebelled sometimes. I love you because you are supremely lovable. I just thought you should know." Lily gives me a hug, and then she stands. "We need to get some sleep."

I nod, unable to speak, and I squeeze her fingers as she heads back to her room. Leaning up, I turn off the light on the end table, and I curl back into the blankets.

Afraid. The word echoes in my ears.

When my mother turned me over, there had been no conversation. The guidance counselor at school had found out I was basically living alone. The police and social services got involved, and everything got messy. When they came to remove me from the "unfit situation," my mother didn't argue with them. All she said to me was, "Go pack your things." I haven't spoken to her since then.

It didn't feel like fear that made me decide to be the perfect foster kid—it felt like survival.

But I had been living like that ever since, always worrying that at any moment everything could be taken from me again. I kept my possessions small, so I could always be ready to move them somewhere else, even as I tried to make myself indispensable to those around me.

Living with Duke and Tabby had been different. Their house felt like a home, like a place I was part of. The article and how Duke reacted, it had seemed to prove how fragile that facade was.

I must have closed my eyes at some point, because the next thing I know, my phone alarm sounds. My limbs feel like spaghetti, but I haul myself up, pulling the sheets off Lily's couch. Lily's already awake and getting dressed, so I head into the bathroom to brush my teeth and do the same.

We get to the hospital early, and I give Lily a long squeeze before we both head back to get prepped. The morning is a flurry of needles, fluids, questions, and breezy hospital gowns. Finally, the nurses wheel me into an operating theater and ask me to count backward from ten.

I wake groggy. There are people around, but I can't make out distinct features. "Thank you," I offer them, but my throat feels like a desert.

Someone pats my shoulder. "You're welcome, sweetheart."

I try to clear my throat, but I wince. "Is Lily okay?" I finally say.

"She's still in surgery but doing great so far. You're both doing great."

I don't realize how much weight lifts off me until I sigh, and my chest feels looser. "That's good. Great."

"Rest, babe," the kind voice says. "We got you."

I drift. When I wake up again, I'm in a darkened space. I can hear beeps, and when I lift my arm, there are still wires and tubes attached. Rubbing my eyes, I attempt to get my bearings. A short woman with glasses appears beside the curtain in front of me. "You're awake." I nod. "Great. Would you like to sit up?" Nodding again, I shift, but the pain in my abdomen stops me. I wince. "Take it slow there. It was laparoscopic, but that's still surgery."

They monitor me for a while. I get word that Lily is in recovery, and the doctor is optimistic about how her surgery went. I'll only be in the hospital for a day or so, but Lily will need to stay longer.

They transport me to a room right before dinner. After I'm settled, my nurse gets me some food and pain medicine. "Are you up for visitors?" She asks when I've swallowed my pills.

Tilting my head, I shift to relieve some discomfort. "I guess?" I don't know who is here, because I already answered a text from Violet. She said she planned to stop in to see me at lunch tomorrow.

The nurse nods, finishes checking my monitors, and leaves. A minute later, there's a tap on my door.

Duke stands in the doorway, his hands in his pockets. I blink a few times to make sure I'm not imagining him, but he's still there. "Hey," he says.

I shift, trying to sit up straighter. I run a hand over my hair. It's pulled into a ponytail that hangs over my shoulder, but I can tell it's probably a mess. "Hey."

"May I come in?" He motions to the chair next to my bed. I nod, and he settles next to me. His gaze travels the length of me. He looks tired, his eyes red. "How are you?"

"I'm okay, I think. A little sore." I study him. "What are you doing here, Duke?" He glances at his hands, and I realize that might have come off harsh. I clear my throat and try again. "It's good to see you. But don't you have practice? Is Tabby okay?"

"She's great. With Nancy." He meets my gaze. "I just needed to see you. Make sure you're okay." He gives a half smile, but it doesn't get to his eyes. "I didn't want to be anywhere else today."

I can't keep from touching him. Reaching for his hand, I cover his fingers with mine. "Thank you. For coming to see me."

He swallows. "Of course." He squeezes my hand, and his eyes roam the room like he doesn't know where to look. "Listen, I know you're tired. I just wanted to see you, to be sure…"

"I love you," I blurt out. His gaze darts to mine. I grip his hand so tightly that I'm afraid I'm hurting him. "I love you, Duke." He opens his mouth, but nothing comes out. Emotions sweep over his features, and I try to define them. Surprise, hope, something infinitely precious. "I am sorry. I should have been more upfront with you. But I wasn't trying to hurt you. It's just hard for me."

His thumb rubs against my knuckles. He reaches forward and brushes a thumb against my cheek. It's only then that I realize there are tears on my face. "What's hard?"

"Trusting people." My voice is raspy, and I don't think it's just from my surgery. "I've been afraid to trust you. To trust that maybe you might love me, even when I'm harder to love."

"You're not hard to love at all, Freckles." He chuckles. "You're a fucking ray of sunshine."

I scowl at him. "I can be super independent, closed off. I'm used to relying on myself. It might take me some time to learn how to be different."

"Whatever you are is just right." He moves to sit next to me. "I'm not perfect either, Freckles. We've already established I don't ask for help well. We'll work it out. And I'm sure there will be other things that come up. But I want to do this with you. I want to be with you, to go through this together." He cups my face, staring into my eyes. "I love you, June Harlow. I've missed you."

I reach for him, all my wires and tubes still attached, and he leans forward, covering my mouth sweetly. The kiss is everything I've ever wanted. It's a promise, and it feels like home to me.

Someone clears their throat from the doorway, and we break apart. My nurse scowls at us. "Miss Harlow just had surgery. She needs her rest, sir." Her voice is heavy with disapproval.

"You're right." Duke gently stands. "I'll be back tomorrow, at lunchtime."

"You have practice, don't you?"

He shrugs. "I'm the captain. I decide where it's important for me to be. And tomorrow, at lunchtime, it'll be important to be here." He leans over and kisses my forehead. "I love you, June Harlow. Never doubt that."

"I love you, too, Duke," I whisper back. He squeezes my hand one more time, and then he leaves.

The nurse's sigh draws my attention. She shrugs. "I hate kicking visitors out. Especially when they look like that." She winks at me, and I laugh.

All the energy I have left saps out of me after she finishes checking my vitals. My eyes are heavy, and I dose off. When I wake, I feel a bit more alert, though in more pain. I press the nurse button for some more pain medicine, and as I wait, I check my phone.

There is a text from Duke. *I love you.*

It's short, sweet, and to the point. But it's everything I've ever wanted, and all I need. I respond. *I love you, too.*

Duke

June comes home two days later. She tires easily, and she's in some pain. But her medicine helps. I read all the discharge instructions carefully. We're following them to the letter. I make sure she walks some and rests, just like it says. When I'm not with her, Nancy or Violet are.

By the third day, all of the fussing irritates her. She says she feels good, so she spends a lot of time on her feet, insisting on making dinner. It's not until the next day when she's exhausted and hurting that she admits she might have been wrong. I manage not to say "I told you so" to her face.

I spend a lot of my spare time snuggling with her. Tabby's thrilled to have her back home, and I catch them cuddled up together, too. Nothing fills me with more happiness than coming home to find them curled up in the chairs in the library, reading.

The Tyrants have a week of away games in Canada right before Thanksgiving. I've always hated being away from Tabby, but now it's almost unbearable to be gone. We do video calls and text, but it's not the same. From all indications, June's almost back to normal. The color has returned to her face, and she tells me on the Wednesday before the holiday that she went all day without a nap.

"Pulled an all-dayer, did you?" I tease her as we video chat on our phones. I'm waiting for our plane. We're on the red-eye home. I'm looking forward to spending the holiday with my girls.

"It's practically like a workout." She nods with satisfaction, and I laugh at her. "How's Huck?"

Last night, Huck pulled his right hamstring. "He's sore and bitchy." I've played with Huck for years, but I've never seen him like this.

"How long do they think he'll be out?"

"Not sure yet. They're going to run more tests when they get him back home." I sigh. "If he's out for a while, I'm not sure what we'll do." They're talking about calling up the goalie from our minor team, but we're on a winning streak. We need someone formidable in the net, and I don't know if the kid from the minors is ready.

"I can't wait to see you."

"Me, too, Freckles. I've missed you like hell."

"Same." She smiles, and I love the warmth in her eyes. Hell, I love everything about her. "What time does your flight get in?"

"Five o'clock. I should be home around six."

"Okay. I'm going to bed so I can spend as much time as possible with you when you get here."

"I love you, June."

"I love you, too, Duke."

The flight gets delayed, though, thanks to some snow in Vancouver, and I don't pull into the driveway until almost ten the next morning. Though I only managed a few hours of sleep on the plane, I'm wide away as I hurry inside.

The smell of turkey hits my nostrils, and I breathe deeply. "I'm home," I call.

"Daddy!" Tabby races from the kitchen and hits me at a run. I sweep her up, twirling her around. I'm not sure if it's possible, but I think she's grown since I left.

She's also covered in flour. "What are you doing?"

"Apple pie," she answers. Her face glows. "It's June's recipe."

"Of course it is." I kiss her cheek. We're still waiting for some of her testing to come back, but they've discovered she has dysgraphia. It's a disorder characterized by writing disabilities. This past week, she worked with an occupational therapist. Her teachers and June seem hopeful about therapy's ability to help her.

I carry my daughter into the kitchen. June's drying her hands, and when she turns to face us, her face lights up. She joins us, wrapping her arms around us both. My universe contracts. These two people are the most important things.

"I've told your girl to take it easy," Nancy says, coming out of the living room. "She's a stubborn one." She shakes her head at June, but I don't miss the affection on her face. I wouldn't have expected them to become close, especially after their first meeting ended so badly. But they seem to have bonded since then over their love for Tabby. I'm not surprised Nancy came around. It's hard not to fall in love with my June.

June throws up her hands in surrender. "I promised I'd take breaks. This crust is almost done."

"Then you'll sit down?" Nancy lifts her eyebrows.

"I promise." She crosses a finger over her heart.

Nancy sniffs, but she pats June's cheek and ruins the effect. Then she points toward the living room. "Tabby, did you want to watch some of the parade with me?"

"Go ahead," June tells my daughter. "I've got the pie."

"Okay." Tabby follows Nancy into the other room, talking about which balloons are on the parade route next.

Alone, I gather June against me. "Hi," I say.

"Hey, you," she responds. Lifting on tiptoes, she wraps her arms around my neck and places her lips on mine. "Guess what?"

"What?" I whisper, my mouth playing across hers. I don't think I'll ever get enough of the taste of this woman.

"I was thinking, if you're up to it, that we might spend some quality time together later tonight." She leans back a few inches and wiggles her brows at me.

"Are you propositioning me, Freckles?" I tease.

"I am." She nods, kissing me again. "Is it working?"

"Baby, trust me. You'll never have to try too hard." I sweep forward and capture her mouth. As our lips meld together, I breathe her in. There's nowhere in the world I'd rather be than kissing a flour-covered June Harlow in my kitchen. "But are you sure you're healed enough? I don't want to do anything that might hurt you." As much as I want to make love to her again, there's no way I'll risk hurting her or setting back her recovery.

"The glue has dissolved. I feel good. If we take it slow…"

Tabby comes tearing in, and June stiffens in my arms. "Daddy! June! Santa is coming. He's in the parade!" She leaves as fast as she arrived, and June's head falls to my chest as she drowns in giggles.

"Hey, June," I whisper in her ear. She shivers. "Did you hear? Santa's coming."

She presses her lips to my cheek and then whispers back, "I hope we are tonight, too."

I chuckle and squeeze her hand before I pull away.

The day progresses in a flurry of perfect celebration. We eat early, and June and I curl up on the couch to watch football. I'm pretty sure we both doze off while Nancy keeps Tabby company. Later, we snack on leftovers and eat pie. At around six o'clock, Nancy stands and declares, "I'm exhausted. I'm going to head home." She glances at June and me. "How about I keep Tabby at my place tonight? What do you think, girly?" She asks.

Tabby squeals and heads upstairs to pack a bag before I can even say anything. No doubt she's already looking forward to a late night and too many sweets.

"Nancy..." I start.

"Why don't you and June get some rest tonight?" She offers, her eyebrows high. "I'll bring Tabby back tomorrow. She's on vacation after all."

I pull June against my side. "Thank you."

Half an hour later, they're gone, and I sweep June into my arms. I lower my lips to hers, and she curls her fingers in the hair at the nape of my neck. Jet lag pulls at me, but I push it aside and carry her upstairs to my room.

I'm as gentle as I can be when I set her in the center of the blankets. I refuse to take any chances with her. With infinite care, I remove her clothes. Her incisions are still red, even angry around the edges, and I place the softest kisses next to them before I kiss my way across her skin. It's been weeks since I've held her like this, and I refuse to rush. By the time I strip out of my own clothes, the color is high on her cheeks, and I'm convinced I've paid proper attention to every freckle on her gorgeous body. "I love you," I tell her.

She places her palms on each side of my face. "I love you, too."

I join our bodies, and we cry out together. Maybe I flew in on a plane this morning, but being here with June is my real homecoming.

When we come back down, I'm careful as I gather her next to me. "Are you okay?"

"I'm perfect." She sighs. "I missed you."

I press a kiss on her temple. "Me, too." After a quick trip to the bathroom, we curl up together again, and I pull the blankets up. Neither of us says anything for a while, but I don't sleep. Instead, I revel in holding her against me.

"Duke?" Her voice surprises me. She's so relaxed against me, I almost thought she dozed off.

"Yeah?"

"I need to talk to you about something." She turns in my arms. In the dim light, I hold her gaze and brush strands of red hair from her face. I love looking at her. "I'm going to take the substitute job at Tabby's school."

My hand stills where I've been drawing circles on her back. "You are?" She told me last week that she'd send in her resume and application.

She nods. "The principal called me this week. She said that she didn't need to interview me and that Tabby's teacher's recommendation was enough for her. It's only for a maternity leave, but Miss Shepherd said the teacher might stay out the rest of the year. And it would give me some experience to find something permanent next year."

I weigh my words. "Do you want to take the job?"

She nods again. "I do." She pauses, swallowing. "And I think I should move in with Violet permanently. This has nothing to do with us. I love being here with you. But Tabby..." She lets her voice trail off.

"I see." My mind races. "Can you hold on for a minute?" I shift, sliding out from under the covers. I don't bother with my boxers. Crossing the room, I open the suitcase I took to Canada and shuffle around in it.

"Duke?" June sits up in bed, pulling the blankets up over her breasts. "Did you hear me? I was saying I should move out."

"Yep. I heard you. Just hang on." When I find what I was looking for, I return to the side of the bed and turn on the lamp on the nightstand. June smooths her hair out of her face, confusion on her features. "But before we discuss that, I wanted to talk to you about something, too."

I drop to my knee next to her. Her mouth opens with a gasp. "June," I begin. "I know we had an unorthodox beginning, but I want all of your beginnings and endings from here on." I pull out the ring I bought when I was in Vancouver. It's a gorgeous round solitary set in a classic four-prong setting. Her eyes are as wide and round as quarters. "I love you. I've known for a long time that I want to marry you, that I want to share my whole life with you. You can teach or not, whatever you want. You can even move back with Violet if you prefer. If you aren't ready to say yes, that's okay. But I need you to know this is what I want. I want to marry you, to spend my life with you. To have you in my bed. To raise Tabby and any other children we have with you. I'm all in with you, and I hope you'll do all of this with me."

She lunges forward and wraps her arms around my neck. "I love you, Duke. And I do want to marry you. Yes, yes, yes."

I crawl back into bed with less finesse than might be expected from a hockey player, and I kiss her deeply.

When I pull back, she's flushed with happiness. "But I still want to teach."

I nod immediately. "Then you should. You're going to be amazing at it. I want you to be happy."

"Thank you."

I slide the ring on her finger, and we kiss again. That leads to us making love again. This time, though, we sleep when we finish.

She isn't next to me when I wake up the next morning. I check the clock, and it turns out it's almost noon. Jet lag is a beast.

I climb out of bed, put on some clothes, and head off to find her. She's curled up in a reading chair in the library, a cup of coffee next to her and her computer in her lap. I lean down to kiss her cheek. "Morning, Freckles."

"Good morning." She smiles up at me and then turns the computer screen toward me. "You mentioned having children last night?" She scoots over to make room for me on the oversized chair. It's a tight fit, though, so I pull her onto my lap. When we're settled, she shows me the screen.

"Department of Children and Families," I read. "What's this?"

"It's the requirements to be foster parents." Suddenly, she looks uncertain. "I thought we could consider fostering. Until we're ready to have more children of our own."

I squeeze her. "I don't know anything about it. Tell me more."

"It's straightforward. The approval process. And since we have so much space here..." She talks fast, a sure sign she's anxious. "It's just that there are so many kids who need safe places, and since I've been through it, I thought I'd be a good fit."

I lift my hand. "I'm on board. Just listening to your experiences would convince me. I think this is a great idea."

"You do?" The tentative hope on her face fills me with tenderness.

"Of course, I do." Someday, she'll learn to believe in me automatically. I plan to work to earn that trust every day.

Joy spreads across her face. "Great. We can fill this out, then. Together."

I pull her against me. "Just how I plan to do everything from now on," I say. "Together."

Epilogue
June

We marry in an intimate ceremony right before Christmas. Neither of us see any reason to wait, and I never wanted a big wedding. All I want is Duke and Tabby.

The Tyrants are out of town for the week between Christmas and New Year's Day. Since both Tabby and I are off from school, we travel to the west coast to watch a few of Duke's games. It's my first time on a plane. The team is on a winning streak, and they lead the Eastern Conference. Huck hasn't been able to return to the ice, thanks to his hamstring tear. Our new goalie, Nate Graham, might bother me personally, but he's played spectacularly.

We spend a day in Disneyland.

When we return home, Tabby starts a Learn to Play hockey program hosted through the Tyrants organization.

"I don't like this." Duke stands on the corner, watching his daughter on the ice.

"Watching?" I offer, bundled up beside him. "The program? Hockey?"

He casts me a withering glance before returning his eyes to his daughter. "I wonder if they need any help out there. I could offer... I'd be able to make some of the Saturday morning practices."

"Duke, no." We've already discussed this. "She's fine. Trust me." After we bought Tabby the basketball hoop, it became clear how much she preferred team sports—like her father. Tabby quit dance, and she signed up for girls' rec basketball. Basketball started after Thanksgiving, and she loves it. She's made a few friends, and I feel like it's given her a boost of confidence.

But watching her on the ice? Her face glows. Seems Duke's daughter loves the game as much as he does.

"They should work on skills. Stick handling."

"They will." I glare at him. "But that kid?" I nudge my head toward a boy around Tabby's age who's stuck on his back like an overturned turtle. "Not ready for stick handling."

"But Tabby..."

I turn, wrapping my arms around his neck. He allows the distraction, pulling me against him. I lift onto my tiptoes to kiss him. "Tabby is fine."

He sighs. "I know. But I worry."

I squeeze him again, and my heart couldn't be more full. "Your worrying is one of my favorite things about you." He casts me a dubious look. "Seriously. I know you just want her to be happy. But you need to let her take this journey alone." I can't imagine how intimidating it would be to have the captain of a professional hockey team as a father while trying to learn to hold a hockey stick.

"I know." He drops another kiss on my lips, and we turn together to watch Tabby again. Her brow furrows as she concentrates on moving the puck forward.

My phone buzzes in my coat pocket. When I retrieve it, it's the number of the social worker we've been working with. "It's Katie," I tell Duke. He nods as I answer. "Hi, Katie. How are you?"

"I'm good, June. But I need your help."

"Of course."

"I have a one-year-old girl who needs somewhere today. I have her now. Can you help?"

I glance up at Duke. He overheard, or he assumes the reason for Katie's call. Either way, he's already nodding. "Yes," I tell her. "Where can we meet her?"

"Where are you?"

"I'm at the hockey rink, the training center, watching Tabby practice."

"Can I bring her there?"

"Of course. Whatever you need." My head spins. I don't have a crib, but I'm sure Lily has a pack-and-play we can borrow. Now that she's recovering back at her home, it'll be a quick stop to pick it up. She'll be happy to help.

"I'll see you in fifteen minutes."

We disconnect, and I glance at the phone in my hand. Then I meet Duke's gaze. "We have our first foster child."

"Yes, we do. Did I hear her say she's a one-year-old?" The sorrow on his face matches my own. It's heartbreaking to consider family separations like this.

I nod, and then I swallow, suddenly overwhelmed by uncertainty. "I'm nervous."

He kisses my cheek. "That makes sense. You care. I'm nervous, too. But she needs us."

"She does." I focus on that.

Duke pulls me against him. "We got this. Together."

"Together," I say, and I believe it.

About the Author

JOSIE BLAKE WRITES CONTEMPORARY romance with sass and emotion. Originally from a small town in western Pennsylvania, she now battles traffic in southern New Jersey where she lives with her hero husband and their happily-ever-after: two very energetic sons. When she isn't writing, she can be found next to a hockey rink or swimming pool, cooking up something sweet, or hiding from encroaching dust bunnies with a book. She loves to hear from readers so please feel free to drop her a note or visit her website at josieblake.com. Connect with her on Instagram at instagram.com/josieblakeauthor, or on Facebook at Facebook.com/JosieBlakeAuthor

Made in United States
Troutdale, OR
01/14/2024

16945786R00139